THE GARGOYLE AFFAIR

AN ENCHANTED ROCK IMMORTALS NOVELLA

Stephanie –
Happy Reading!
Amanda

Be sure to get all of Amanda's exciting stories, available exclusively through Kindle and Kindle Unlimited!

The Enchanted Rock Immortals World

The Puma's Second Chance—FREE!
The Wolf Shifter's Redemption
The Demon's Shifter Mate
The Fae's Obsession
The Shifter's Savior
The Lion Shifter's Trust
The Gargoyle Dilemma
The Demon's Choice
The Vampire's Vendetta
The Fae's Future
The Wolf's Mage
The Shifter's Sorcerer
Immortal Conspiracy: An Enchanted Rock Immortals Box Set
Immortal Intrigue: An Enchanted Rock Immortals Box Set
Immortal Seduction: An Enchanted Rock Immortals Box Set

The Flannigan Sisters Psychic Mysteries

Finders Keepers
Ghosts, Pies, & Alibis
Murder Most Merry
Fourth and Long
Ghosts, MOs, & a Baking Show
Last Rodeo
Crash and Burn
Gossip, Ghosts, and Grudges
Seasons Slayings

The Enchanted Rock Immortals World

Releases by Author

Eve Cole

Avian
The Dragon's Phoenix
Alpha
Anomaly
The Mate Maker
The Rook's Mate
The Shifter's Assassin
The Shifter's Thief
Avian, Anomaly, The Rook's Mate:
An Enchanted Rock Immortals Novella M/M Box Set
The Dragon's Phoenix, Alpha, the Mate Maker:
An Enchanted Rock Immortals Novella M/F Box Set

Fenley Grant

Sorcery, Snakes, and Scorpions: A Love Story
Witches, Werewolves, and War: A Love Story
Unwed, Unfed, and the Undead: A Love Story
Curses, Cats, and Crime: A Love Story
Pinwheels, Potions, and Possibilities: A Love Story
Twists, Turns, and Telekinetics: A Love Story
Aliases, Artifacts, and Attraction: A Love Story
Rings, Rituals, and Rock & Roll: A Love Story
Mistletoe, Merriment, and Murder: A Love Story
Moonlight, Magic, and Mayhem: A Clan Magic Box Set, Vol. 1
Moonlight, Magic, and Mayhem: A Clan Magic Box Set, Vol. 2
Moonlight, Magic, and Mayhem: A Clan Magic Box Set, Vol. 3

Robin Lynn

Of Magic, Love, and Fangs
The Demon King's Runaway Bride

Susan Person

Fae Undone

Fae Redone

Amanda Reid

The Puma's Second Chance—FREE!

The Wolf Shifter's Redemption

The Demon's Shifter Mate

The Fae's Obsession

The Shifter's Savior

The Lion Shifter's Trust

The Gargoyle Dilemma

The Demon's Choice

The Vampire's Vendetta

The Fae's Future

The Shifter's Sorcerer

The Wolf's Mage

The Shifter's Sorcerer

Immortal Conspiracy: An Enchanted Rock Immortals Box Set

Immortal Intrigue: An Enchanted Rock Immortals Box Set

Immortal Seduction: An Enchanted Rock Immortals Box Set

Sharla Wylde

A Mermaid's Choice—FREE!

A Mermaid's Quest

A Merman's Mission

A Mermaid's Rescue

Atlantis Revealed: An Enchanted Rock Immortals Box Set

All titles available exclusively in Kindle and Kindle Unlimited

THE GARGOYLE AFFAIR

AN ENCHANTED ROCK IMMORTALS NOVELLA

AMANDA REID

ISBN: 978-1-951770-20-4

For every new beginning, something must end.

THE ENCHANTED ROCK IMMORTALS

Demons and Vampires. Elves and Fairies. Mages and Witches. Werewolves and Dragons. Psychics and Telekinetics.

These magical beings and more exist, rubbing shoulders in their daily lives with unsuspecting humans. But a supernatural society doesn't happen without order. Millennia ago, the Clans —Sanguis, Fae, Magic, Shifter, and Human Paranormal— wisely formed a Council to maintain that order. The end? To ensure the worlds of human and paranormal beings didn't collide and break out into a war that would result in the extermination or subjugation of either.

As human civilization progressed, the first council formed the All Clan Charter at the natural vortex in Great Zimbabwe, giving each clan a voice in the administration of affairs both between the clans and with humans. Next, Asia formed its council at Chengtu Vortex. Then European at Warel Chakra Vortex. North America came next at the natural vortex humans called Enchanted Rock, in what today is known as Texas.

Now, thriving communities of paranormal beings exist in

and around the granite outcropping. Humans scrabble over the dome, not suspecting an entire city exists within its confines: the North American Council and all its departments —Legislative, Administrative, Security, Medical, Vortex Transportation, and Legal, plus restaurants, clan hotels, and shops catering to the paranormal crowds.

Also under that dome? Intrigue, politics, and most importantly, love.

These are the stories of The Enchanted Rock Immortals.

CHAPTER 1

Movement in her peripheral vision caught Tabitha McBee's attention, and she put her phone back in the store's cash wrap's drawer, disappointed she'd have to wait again to order her salad. A steady stream of customers meant her lunch would come late today, if at all.

She added a warm, welcoming smile to her features and pivoted to greet Boutique Magique's next customer.

Instead of someone in search of chic women's clothing, Fernald Grayson opened the door and stepped across the threshold.

She eyed the tall gargoyle and tried to ignore the little skip of her heart. Sure, he was good looking. Most paranormals were, especially the fae. In this case, Fernald was perhaps the most handsome being she'd ever seen with his wavy black hair, intense gray eyes, square jaw, and muscles stacked on muscles. If she decided purely on physicality, she would've totally gone for someone like him, but his standoffish attitude and muttered comments about "duty" made her want to yawn. She'd assigned him his logo—tall, dark, and boring.

But is he really? You barely know him. The notion put a hitch in her step, especially when her thoughts swerved to getting to know him better and where "knowing" might lead.

Nope. She'd been down that road, and the toll was way too high.

"Good afternoon, Tabitha." He stopped in the main aisle before the table loaded with sweaters. "Just checking in."

She wanted to fidget under his steady gaze, but she straightened her spine. "Everything's fine. No sign of Lord Regus or a minion."

A barely perceptible tightening of Fernald's broad shoulders made Tabby wish she'd hadn't added her second sentence. The elf lord who threatened her boss's business had once indentured Fernald. Luckily, North American Council Security put the evil fae behind bars for helping manage one of the most pernicious crime syndicates in the paranormal world. Yet, the maximum-security prison built to house all the clans—Sanguis, Magic, Fae, Shifter, or Human Paranormal—had been beaten before. Lord Regus, who disapproved of his son's marriage, had directed his ire at Thelma, the boutique's owner, for helping his new daughter-in-law with her wedding dress. Fernald kept a loose watch on Thelma and the store while his brother, also Thelma's boyfriend, was away on Hebert Security business.

Tabby broke the awkward silence that had formed. "Well, um, I think we're good."

The door behind Fernald opened, and a tall woman with gorgeous, caramel-streaked, dark blonde hair and rich, tanned skin walked through the opening. A Jaguar shifter if Tabby had ever seen one.

Fernald immediately pivoted his position to observe the newcomer, and his hands came up to waist-level.

The woman's bright green gaze swept the gargoyle while

she sauntered forward. With a smile worthy of a hungry predator sizing up a meal, she said, "Hellooo, Handsome."

Tabby discounted the small pang as merely annoyance that he hadn't left yet so she could help her customer without the attractive distraction. Nope, not jealous at all that he kept his gaze on the female. Nor was she gratified by Fernald's impassive features when he added a brief nod while he said, "Madam." He turned to Tabby. "Let me know if you need me."

Heat began to creep up from her middle with his intense focus and low, rumbly words. Her equanimity needed him gone.

With the uncomfortable knowledge she'd lied to herself about how he affected her causing the warmth to gild her cheeks, Tabby nodded, then turned her most welcoming smile to the customer.

"How can I help you?"

~

Tabby handed the boutique's branded hanging bag to the beautiful sorcerer. "Here you go. You're going to knock everyone out at the party."

"Thanks for staying a little late for me tonight." Lauren Williams's smile glowed against her flawless, light brown skin. She hooked the hangers over her finger, then swung the bundle around so the garments hung behind her shoulder. "I've been looking for the perfect dress, and I should've known I'd find it here."

Tabby grinned with the praise since the other woman always had fabulous style. She unlocked the door, which she'd secured earlier, then pulled the opening wide for her customer. "You know we're always open for you."

"Tell Thelma I'm sorry I missed her, and hopefully, I'll see you both at the party." Lauren added a breezy wave as she exited. Without a backward glance, she strode down the short side street and onto the broad pedestrian walkway. With her confident pace, she rounded the corner of the bank and out of sight in short order.

Inside, Tabby glowed. An invitation to Lauren's Christmas bash was definitely a score, especially two months from the event.

Movement from the corner of her eye drew Tabby's attention. She scanned the shadows across from her. First Bank of Enchanted Rock's facade could've been a temple to the financial gods with all the thick columns carved from the native pink granite ringing its building. The spelled ceilings of Enchanted Rock's promenade level had dipped to twilight to mimic the outside world. The shadow's murk under the bank's eaves would've precluded her from seeing a troll standing between the building and columns.

For a moment, a patch of inky blackness seemed to move, and she tensed, then reminded herself Fernald lurked in the area.

Ugh. Probably just him.

Tabby threw the bolt once more, annoyed that her lady bits liked the idea the gargoyle might be close.

The lamp on the avenue's corner flared to life, and she peeked at her watch. Six-thirty already. Rats. Well, at least if she had to stay late, she sacrificed her non-existent social life for a client with a snarky sense of humor and great fashion sense.

She glanced around at the state of the racks. With holiday parties already on people's calendars and winter styles arriving regularly, the store had a steady business today. Since she'd be off work for a couple of days, she couldn't leave this mess for Thelma.

While she straightened, her wayward mind kept wandering back to Fernald and how she'd reacted earlier when the gorgeous jaguar shifter eyed him like a prime cut of meat. Tabby had been jealous, plain and simple.

She snorted a laugh and set the hanger back in place with a little more force than necessary. Broke and divorced didn't make for a good resume, even if she wanted to date. Which she definitely didn't.

Perhaps with Fernald hanging around, her ex-husband would be less likely to show up and harass her for money, not that she had any to share, thanks to him. The hawt gargoyle could serve some purpose even if not satisfying her libido.

Finally, she surveyed her work with a critical eye. Everything appeared to be in order, and she'd closed out the sales for the day.

Her stomach grumbled. Food. She'd missed lunch and needed to fill the hollow. While she considered her options to pick up on the way home, she darted into the back room to grab her oversized purse, then dimmed the lights, activated the wards, and stepped outside. The burrito place was on the way to the parking level. That'd be enough for a couple of meals and good for her tighter finances.

She wrapped her fingers around her purse's handles and hurried down the walkway. At the promenade, she merged with the pedestrians from the business day who'd started to frequent the dining establishments. She glanced at the Werehouse along the way and her stomach mumbled a yearning. Nope. The expensive steak restaurant's price didn't fit into her strict budget.

Not that her job at the boutique paid poorly, and not that she didn't appreciate Thelma for giving her a spot to land after she'd been fired, but the hourly wage just couldn't make up for what Tabby had earned as a partner in an advertising agency.

Plus, the legal fees for the divorce and the resulting upside-down house sale had practically wiped her out financially. Hopefully, she'd land one of the three job prospects she had lined up, and her bank account could once again manage a steak from—

She bounced against something and landed on her ass with a thump that traveled in a lightning jolt from her tailbone to the top of her spine. Momentum carried her backward, and she hit her head on the unforgiving granite. Stars swam in front of her, and she couldn't catch her breath to utter a sound or have a coherent thought.

A mumbled, "Sorry about that, here's your purse," came from above in a familiar voice. The footsteps hurried off.

"Stop." The authoritative word came from over her shoulder some distance away and sounded suspiciously like Fernald.

The shape of the man who hit her came into focus, but his long, paranormally-fast strides had taken him at least fifty yards away toward one of the parking exits. Tall, with a slim physique and brown hair, he'd dressed in black pants and a long-sleeved T-shirt. He could've been anyone in the paranormal community.

What a jerk to hit and run. She closed her eyes against the streetlamp's harsh glare, which hadn't appeared all that bright earlier.

A wave of dizziness shifted her surroundings. She brought her hand to the back of her head and massaged the throbbing area. Concussion? Probably. She'd had one once when she played softball in high school and knew the signs.

Booted feet appeared in her peripheral vision, then black tactical-pant-clad knees.

With a grimace she lifted her lids and glanced up.

Fernald.

"I saw that male run into you. Are you okay?" Concern creased the corners of his bright blue eyes and pinched his lips. His gaze shot to her legs then back up, but now his angular cheeks were stained a dull red against his olive-toned skin.

What? Her gaze fell to her skirt which had ridden up her thighs to the point where the nubby wool barely covered her crotch. Heat bloomed in her cheeks. At least she'd worn tights today against the unseasonably cool Texas weather. She tugged at the fabric until her modesty recovered.

"I think I'm okay. Just bruised pride." She straightened her spine, then her blouse. In preparation to rise, she rearranged her feet. Her head pulsed with the movements, and a small moan slipped from her lips before she could stop the tell-tale sign.

"You sure you don't want to stay down? That granite had to hurt." He settled his hand on her shoulder briefly, then pulled away, almost as if he was afraid to touch her.

"I'm fine." She said the words through gritted teeth more for her benefit than his. Somehow, she managed a wan smile. "I could use help up, though."

His large hands and steadying presence centered her while she carefully regained her footing. Though she hadn't broken anything, her body felt heavy, like each pound she carried had doubled.

When her knees wobbled, he brought his hand to her elbow. "Steady. I can call med services if you want."

After a hefted breath, she favored him with what she hoped appeared as a grateful expression because she welcomed his solid, calm demeanor. "Thanks, I'm fine."

He met her smile, then bent to retrieve the tote-sized bag she called a purse. "I think this is yours."

Ugh. The leather satchel seemed to weigh more than ever too. Probably just a result of her fall. She fitted the handles over her shoulder, determined to just get to her car. She listed a little, then with his help again, remained upright.

"If you're sure you don't want me to call the medics, can I at least drive you home?" The deep baritone of his voice remained carefully neutral.

She may have hit her head hard, but she could still comprehend his reasoning. The way the throbbing pain at the back of her head had moved to her temples, along with the trembling of her limbs, seemed to indicate she would be better off with someone else driving. She couldn't call Thelma, because she'd travel for thirty minutes from her house in Illusion. Nor could Tabby call her friend Yvette, because she'd be almost an hour away on the outskirts of Austin. None of her less close friends lived at the Rock and would have to drive in too.

Which left Fernald. She glanced up to the handsome, capable gargoyle next to her, and her stomach did a little flip that kept her speechless.

"If you don't want me to, I understand. I can wait with you while someone comes to pick you up." His tone carried a hint of disappointment, but otherwise, no deception, just sincerity to her paltry empathic skills.

Good grief. Either this guy was yet one more con artist or she should jump on him as one of the last of the good ones. The throb in her temples suggested that she should leave now.

"Okay, but wait a minute." She pulled her phone from the purse's zippered pocket on the front, then fired off a text to her boss that she fell, hit her head, was okay, and that Fernald would be taking her home.

Someone should know her plans. As her ex-husband, or as

she liked to call him, her was-band, had shown, her pitiful empathic senses were easily misled.

She didn't wait for a reply and slid the phone back into its pocket. Her hunger might have disappeared, but she needed to bring something back since she hadn't been grocery shopping for weeks.

"Ready. But I need to get a burrito first."

CHAPTER 2

An enticing, spicy aroma rose from the bag he held and mixed with the garage's vehicle exhaust, but all Fernald could focus on was the alluring scent of the woman who passed him while he held the exit door for her. Honeystars, one of the exotic blooms from the fae realm, couldn't smell sweeter or more lush than the perfume Tabitha wore.

He resisted taking a deep breath to imprint the smell in his memory. Tabitha, or Tabby as many called her, existed so far out of his league that he found himself flustered and stumbling like a youth faced with his crush. His cheeks grew warm yet again for at least the tenth time since he'd witnessed the man practically mow her down, then run off. He shifted his thoughts away from the sheer amount of leg he'd been afforded.

She was hurt, you dolt and you only gaped? And you let the man escape after harming her. Like you're watching her ass now instead of scanning for threats.

"What level are you on?" Her question caught his thoughts and the butterflies bouncing around in him went faster. She'd halted, turned, and waited for him.

Level? He hurriedly caught up both in wits and distance. "I don't have a car."

"How are you getting me home then?" Tightness formed brackets around her mouth and eyes, though without animus. She must still be in pain from her head striking the ground. Humans were incredibly fragile compared to gargoyles.

"I thought I'd drive your car. I can fly back once I drop you off."

Her tight features eased, and she massaged her forehead. "Oh. I didn't consider that. And here I thought I was making logical decisions."

When she pivoted to continue toward the elevator, he fell into step with her. "Do I need to get you a MendMe potion before we leave?"

"I've got some at the house."

He'd never used one because his lord had never deemed his soldiers worthy of the expense. Though he'd heard the earlier she took the potion the better, he'd defer to her judgement. The sounds around him bounced off the granite, the door slams from cars, people talking, and vehicles coming and going. None appeared threatening, yet the odd feeling of doom lingered. He pushed the button to call the elevator, then took the position that would provide him the best view both of his surroundings and her should she have another wobbly moment.

While he waited with her, then rode down two floors and followed her to her car, he tried to wall off his reaction to her proximity. The problem with gargoyles is that the fae who made them insisted on their creations having little ability to withstand mental intrusion. He'd learned early to hide his emotions behind a mask of duty, but as an empath, she still might pick up on the way she made him feel—hungry and untamed.

Besides, she didn't appear to return his interest at all. Instead, he'd do what he could to keep her safe by maintaining his vigilance. Only once did he think he saw a shadow in the corner of his eye, but when he turned his attention, nothing seemed to be amiss.

She stopped in front of a large, black SUV and she turned to him. "Hey. Are you sure you want to do this?"

Had he been too forward? Maybe he'd made her uncomfortable. "Of course. Why?"

"It's just that…nothing." A spasm crossed her face.

Instead of folding her into his arms like he wished, he said, "You seem to be in pain, and I'd feel better if you'd let me drive. Would you prefer I didn't?"

Her mouth tightened, then she blew out a quick breath and turned toward the passenger side of the SUV. "You're just really quiet. I'm not used to the silence."

"*If I want to hear what you think, I'll ask a troll,*" was more often than not the rebuke when he'd voice his opinion to his father. Fernald typically sucked back a bitter response. Father had pompously adopted the phrase from the fae lord who'd once indentured them. The same one to whom Fernald now owed no loyalty, thank the gods.

Yet, she wasn't the same as the fae Fernald had once served. Transitioning to being more than a tool to be wielded against enemies challenged him more than he'd expected. His conversational skills needed more effort. "My apologies. I was concentrating on ensuring your safety."

Since most things on this plane weren't made to withstand a gargoyle's strength, he pulled on the SUV's handle gently, but the door didn't budge.

"No apology needed, but what are you saving me from?" Her voice came from the other side of the SUV. Its darkened windows gave him a shadow of her silhouette. "Where are you?"

"At the driver's side. Can you unlock it?"

Her musical laughter proceeded her reply. "That's not my car."

Shit. Embarrassment fueled his pace around the back end of the SUV to where she stood next to a compact two-door sedan, which had been backed into the space. The car had probably seen as many years as he had. Well, maybe not ninety-five, but certainly that old in car years. The silver finish had started to go chalky on the hood and a chink in the windshield had begun to spiderweb. Those features paled in comparison to the miniature size.

A laugh, this time one that held little amusement, turned him from the assessment. She cocked her head to one side. "Maybe I should've warned you ahead of time that my ride wouldn't be up to your standards or size."

Though the fae were often proud creatures, gargoyles typically didn't have that luxury. Instead of harping on yet another way his life had sucked, he went for humor. In a deadpan tone, he said, "I don't even own a car yet. I have to admire yours."

For a moment, he didn't think she'd respond, but then she widened her eyes and favored him with another of her intoxicating laughs, one which told him he'd inspired genuine amusement and caused warmth to blossom in his cold, stony heart. She climbed into the passenger seat while he crossed to the other side and opened the driver's door.

Even the full-size SUVs were a bit cramped for his six-foot, eight-inch frame. How would he fold himself inside? Standard shift too. If he flexed his elbows to shift gears, he'd probably hit her in the head. Hyperbole, but not by too much.

With one hand, she reached under the driver's seat and the cracked leather seat slid back. She dipped her head until she met his gaze where he'd bent to try to figure out how he'd cram himself into the tiny compartment. His blood felt a little fizzy with the teasing light in her eyes. "That's as far as it goes, I'm afraid. I can't reach the lever to recline the back, but that might help too."

He eyed the lever. Maybe.

"I'll understand if you need to pass." Her words came out in a rush. "Thanks for staying with me. I'll be okay to the house."

Mouse would never forgive him if she came to harm. Fernald almost snorted a laugh. Who was he kidding. His half-brother had nothing to do with his decision. "I can get in."

He depressed the lever until he'd almost fully reclined the back, then somehow managed to fold himself into the car. He ducked to avoid direct contact with the headliner, which had begun to sag in places. He splayed his knees in order to both avoid the steering wheel as well as operate the accelerator, brake, and clutch. One hundred pounds of flour stuffed in a fifty-pound sack would fit better.

"Here's the key." Using her thumb, she depressed a little button on the fob she held out and a thin, engraved metal bar swung out.

Huh. He hadn't seen one of those in a while. Most of the gargoyles were merely foot soldiers. Wings and feet met their transportation needs. Luckily, Fernald had risen to his lord's security detail and therefore had a reason to know how to drive and could operate a standard shift. The fae often had business outside the realm of Lanorinia, and elves couldn't access every location by ley line or vortex, necessitating this primitive form of travel.

He accepted the key and closed the door. The engine fired up with no indication the parts matched the exterior's age.

"My grandma made sure to keep her car engines in top

shape, even if she didn't do the same for the paint. Or the interior for that matter."

Dammit. He shouldn't have let down his guard enough for her to notice his surprise. Someone's possessions weren't a reflection on their value, of that he knew well. Gargoyles never had possessions because they could easily be taken by their lord.

He minded his elbow when he put the car in gear and pulled out of the parking spot toward the garage exit. "This was your grandmother's car?"

"Yes. She passed away a couple of years back and after my di—" She sucked in a harsh breath and remained silent for several moments. Then she cleared her throat and said, "About the same time my divorce was finalized, I inherited her car and home."

The brittle tone in her words belied her calm exterior. She turned her head toward the window. "Good thing too. Archer—he's my ex—cleaned out our bank account before he disappeared. Sold the house out from under me with forged documents too. I had to sell my car because I couldn't afford the loan payments. Then he reappeared and contested the divorce, making allegations I had stolen ideas from other people in an attempt to make me settle." Her light tone carried a bitter, razor's edge and a hefty dose of defensiveness. "My agency let me go, so this is my ride now."

He could practically taste the hot, acid fury in her words. Though he'd learned much from glancing interactions at Hebert Security gatherings and from conversations with Mouse and Thelma, he hadn't been aware of her trials. Usually, she seemed bright and shiny. He should know better. The things that burned the brightest were also usually the hottest.

"The judge went on the record to say Archer lied, but by

then…" She cleared her throat, then shook her head like she could scatter her thoughts. "Sorry. I don't often talk about those years. Not exactly fun times."

If the memories brought her pain, she didn't need to satisfy his prurient interest. Meting retribution for Archer's bad deeds would probably be frowned upon anyway. He turned out of the garage and approached the T-intersection to go north or south. "No apology needed. Life is very often not fun." Also a fact all too familiar to him. "Which way?"

"I live on the eastern outskirts of Split. Left, then take Highway 281 north toward Johnson City." She picked at something on her skirt and for several miles remained silent.

He could think of nothing to say that wouldn't sound like a platitude. Instead, he remained mum as well, choosing to focus on the surroundings—wary and watchful.

Headlights bobbed behind in the rearview mirror. Close, but not close enough to make out the type of vehicle beyond new lights, the bright blue kind that tended to blind oncoming traffic. Tension gathered between his shoulder blades. Other than hating the headlights the car behind them employed, he had nothing to explain his sense of danger. Probably lingering worry about the man who accidentally ran into Tabitha.

What had his half-brother said? "*You've been conditioned into a never-ending state of impending threat. You need to let that go once in a while and enjoy yourself.*" After a deep breath, he decided to heed the words and banish the knot coiled in his shoulders.

He glanced toward the woman beside him, who'd been quiet for someone who usually sparkled with confidence and charisma. She'd dropped her gaze and now brushed her thumbs against the knit material encasing her thighs. Hopefully, she hadn't begun to regret him taking her home, or maybe her head hurt more now.

"Hey, you still alright?"

She clutched her thighs. "Yes…and no." Her focus darted to his before her eyelids dropped, shielding the emotion within. "I want to apologize. I forgot there are those who have it far worse than me."

The implication about how gargoyles were treated within the fae realm hit him and he stiffened, returning his attention to the road. "And far worse than me."

He slowed at the intersection with the highway, and a glare cut into his vision through the rearview mirror. The headlights gained on them at an alarming speed and weren't slowing down.

"Shit." He flexed his fingers around the steering wheel. When downshifted, the car engine whined with the effort.

After a gasp, she said, "I'm really so sorry. I won't bring it up ag—"

"Not that." His tone turned gravelly, and his large hand enveloped the gearshift's knob. "We have company."

CHAPTER 3

Still mired in her embarrassment for not just the self-pity party over Archer, but complaining to a gargoyle no less, Tabby didn't grasp Fernald's meaning for a moment. Company?

With a growl, he spun the steering wheel hard.

Her mental cogs still chewed on his meaning, leaving her unprepared for the gravitational yank. She clamped her lips against a scream when her shoulder slammed into the window, and she narrowly avoided a second crack of hard substrate against her skull.

Finally, she comprehended his words. Danger. Then a set of obnoxiously bright headlights flashed in the side mirror.

Tabby closed her eyes in preparation for the jolting grind of metal against metal. Her tiny car's engine whined, and she swore she heard a growl when acceleration pushed her back into her seat.

She popped her eyes open and glanced out the passenger window. While Fernald had turned onto the highway, the other vehicle, a large, black SUV, continued straight and his red taillights disappeared behind the trees lining the highway. How had Fernald avoided that collision?

He shifted the gear and let off of the gas until her car's engine didn't sound like a gang of murder hornets, yet continued zipping through the darkness.

Then her brain began to work. She could've been seriously hurt due to the other driver's actions. She began to shake. First her head and now this—what could possibly be next?

Easy. Just coincidences. No use getting worked up. Let's try some deep breathing. Three deep breaths calmed the worst of her reaction.

"Drivers nowadays suck." Her shaky laugh didn't carry the confidence she'd hoped. Plus, her pulse had spiked, redoubling the throbbing in the back of her head. "That guy would've run into us if you hadn't reacted quickly. Thank you for the second time this evening."

"Welcome." The tight, single word carried a wealth of tension, and she turned to him. The dashboard's illumination limned his chiseled profile, and his gaze seemed to flick from the road to the mirror in rapid alternation. He hadn't let off the gas, either.

"What's wrong?"

He hesitated a long moment before his hand, which had been clutching the gearshift, returned to the steering wheel. The car slowed to a more reasonable rate of speed rather than rocketing along the two-lane stretch. After he flicked a glance to her, he said, "Nothing."

Sure seemed like something. The headlights lit on the green sign for Split and relief sang through her veins. "Take the next right."

Though he made the turn faster than she would have, he made the transition to the blacktopped county road smooth as silk. "You're a good driver. Where'd you learn?"

"One of the skills I needed to obtain for Lord Roundtree."

Dammit. Would she never stop stepping in troll crap? Everything she said seemed to bring his prior life into the conversation. "I'm sorry I brought—"

"Don't be. I had a life that wasn't pretty. That was then. I did my best to protect my family and mitigate the effects Lord Roundtree's orders had on innocents."

Oh my. The bleakness that had crept into his words and the stiff way he held himself once more said she'd stepped in more than troll crap. She'd lit the bag on fire and rang the doorbell. She massaged her temple where the hammers pounded away. Best to just get him to the house and then she could let him go and find peace away from her inexplicable inability to converse without thought.

She silently stewed in her own recriminations until the next turn, which she pointed out to him, and he made a right onto the unpaved county road, his motions economical and compact. How had she missed that he moved his arm carefully in the tight space? That he hadn't knocked her out when he avoided the crash impressed her.

"The next driveway on the left's mine. There."

He pulled off the caliche surface onto the dirt tracks with the ribbon of green between. Smoothly, he stopped the car before going past the rusty barbed wire fence line ringing the property.

"You can go through but stop after, and I'll get out and close the gate." She took a deep breath and tried to infuse some of her grandma's steel into her spine.

The car rolled forward, then he halted the movement and put the car in park. "I'll get it."

The idea he would have to unfold then refold himself back into the car seemed silly. She reached for the door's handle. "I'm fine."

Faster than she could pull the lever, his door opened, and

he had his feet on the ground. Rising to stand seemed as if he executed a deep squat, though his movements were swift and graceful. He bent at his waist and said with a half-smile, "I'll be back in a minute."

A warm glow formed in her stomach. Having someone look out for her when she felt shitty was a luxury. And her head did want to explode. At this point, her stomach protested the idea of the food waiting in the back seat despite her earlier hunger.

He'd impressed her with his consideration. But then Archer had been considerate…at first. Only after the ceremony did he begin to uncloak his narcissistic personality.

Fernald climbed back into the car without a word and started down the long, winding track once more, then through the fence that separated the house from what had once been land cattle grazed. The headlights brushed against the bushes and trees lining the driveway. The house, a blond-brick 1970s ranch concoction came into view.

Despite today's cold snap, Texas's warm temperatures had extended summer into what ordinarily would be early fall. Weeds sprouted from all the planting beds surrounding the house. Thistles, henbit, and bindweed ran wild and several vines snaked their way up the side of the house. Crabgrass sprouted in the carport's concrete. Grandma would be appalled.

First the car, and now what appeared to be a shambles of a house. Just wait until he got inside and saw the dated 1970s interior. Tabby wanted to squirm in her seat but somehow managed to stay still.

She'd been working long hours to satisfy even the modest mortgage she'd inherited, the car insurance, electricity, taxes on the acreage and inheritance, plus the bills for all the other basic joys of modern living, not to mention she'd just paid off the last installment of her divorce attorney's fees. That list alone made her want to cry. When she wasn't working, trying to find a job ate up the rest of her bandwidth. Gardening might be a pastime she loved but was last on her list, right behind cleaning out her grandma's room, something she still hadn't done in the last eighteen months. She didn't even want to think about the barn, which had been packed with more than fifty years of her grandmother's hoarded stuff.

"My gardener quit." She'd blurted out the words, which sounded as panicked as she felt inside. She blinked back the tears threatening, then grabbed for her purse.

"I hear thistles are tough to eliminate. Front door or carport?"

Tabby couldn't decide whether to be relieved or mad that he ignored her obvious fib, or to be intrigued that he knew from the brief flare of the car's headlamps that the spiky, noxious garden invader was extremely hard to eradicate. Why did she care? Damn but her moods were all over the place right now. She leaned her head back against the seat, wincing and jerking away when the tender knot protested contact. "Carport, please."

He guided the tiny car into the shelter and cut the engine. "Let's get you inside, then I can go."

Despite the last two years of declaring to her friends and herself that she'd never need to look at another man across the dining room table, she found she wanted to look at this one. Besides, he'd been considerate and helpful to her and his food *was* in the backseat. "But you haven't eaten dinner yet."

"I can take the burrito with me."

His open posture plus the brief head shake he added to the sincerity in his tone convinced her that he told the truth. Besides, unlike her ex, who she belatedly discovered carried psychic gifts that defeated her own, gargoyles were bred to have a low ability to defend themselves psychically. Reading his emotions shouldn't be a problem.

"Allowing you to have dinner while warm is the least I can do. I've got beer and wine as well." The prospect of having conversation while she ate beyond the single-sided discussion with her cat, made her day seem less depressing. "But if you'd prefer…"

"Thanks." His tone conveyed his surprise. "I'll stay for dinner, but are you sure your head is okay?"

"Once I take the MendMe, I'll be fine." She pulled the handle. When she rose to her feet, her shoulder bag felt heavier than ever, just like her head. Potion first, food possibly later.

She put her hand on the doorknob while she pulled her keys from the front pocket of her purse where she stored them with her phone—otherwise she'd lose them in the tote's vast space. Before she could insert the key into the door, the knob turned.

"Huh."

"What?"

She glanced over her shoulder at the sharp word. "Nothing. Just forgot to lock the door this morning." Funny. She hadn't done that in a long time, but she'd been distracted and running late. She'd need to pay better attention from now on.

After she stepped into the galley kitchen, she flipped on the overhead. The bright fluorescents jammed spikes into her brain. She smothered a gasp. *MendMe. Now.*

Luckily, she'd continued her grandma's practice of putting medications in a kitchen cabinet. She dropped her purse on the counter with a *thunk* and yanked open the cupboard door with a shaking hand.

Only one of the Belladonna Apothecary-prepared potions remained on the shelf, and when she squinted, she found the

"Best by" date had passed last month. Not too bad. But she couldn't seem to budge the top. Dammit.

"Here, let me." He closed the door and put the food bag on the counter next to her.

Biting back a sob-ish growl, she thrust the small, dark bottle toward him.

Despite his large hands, he nimbly removed the top and handed the open vial back.

She accepted the potion thankfully and drained the liquid, uncaring how the oily, foul flavor slicked her tongue and throat. The hammers beat unceasingly, and she needed relief. She looked for the peppermint candy that traditionally came with the potion to relieve the yuck.

Fernald had already unwrapped the lozenge and held the red-striped disk toward her balanced carefully within the clear plastic.

She plucked the candy from his fingers with gratitude since she didn't have to fight the cellophane, and the sugary mint did the usual non-paranormal magic of banishing the nasty funk.

The hammers at her temple began to ease, and she sighed. Though still not hungry by any means, she could probably make a show of eating without nausea now.

She pasted a crescent on her lips that didn't quite match the level of gratitude she felt but was all she could manage. "Thank you."

"You're welcome." The corners of his eyes crinkled with his returned smile and the teal blue glowed, even in the overhead lighting's harsh glare.

Gargoyle eyes are so pretty. Just like the rest of him. She stilled. *Ugh. Put that thought from your head. You just finished paying off your lawyer's bill from the divorce. Your B-O-B can handle anything you need.*

Had the MendMe being out of date somehow lowered her

inhibitions? Sure, some experienced a euphoria, but the potion's known side-effects were few. She pushed the concept aside as two-years of self-imposed celibacy gnawed at her libido when faced with a handsome male. She'd know when the time was right. And she knew better than a gargoyle—any paranormal, for that matter.

Since her nominal psychic gift barely warranted inclusion in the Human Paranormal clan, she'd already determined she'd search in the wider regular population. A normal human wouldn't be able to lie to her like Archer.

Neither would a gargoyle.

CHAPTER 4

While the silence stretched between him and Tabitha in the kitchen, a corresponding itch grew between Fernald's shoulders. He had never been able to explain the ability he'd had to sense danger, but his instinct had never failed him.

Her door had been unlocked.

Right now the itch seemed to be digging a hole into his nearly impenetrable hide. He opened his senses of hearing and smell. Tabitha's heart rate and breathing seemed a bit elevated, but nothing out of the ordinary from someone not feeling particularly well. The disgusting stench of the MendMe lingered, blending with her lovely scent and the spice of the food, plus the faintest whiff of a cat box that no one would otherwise detect.

Nothing seemed out of the ordinary, other than a vague stale odor of the house, strange for the spotless—albeit limited—interior he'd seen. His half-brother had asked him to protect his girlfriend, the shop, and Tabitha while out on assignment for Hebert Security, but Mouse texted an hour ago that he'd returned early. Maybe Fernald should check in with his half-brother to make sure Tabitha's boss hadn't been harmed. Bah. Even that thought felt wrong, like his instinct pushed him in the itchy spot toward the woman in front of him.

Okay. For now, he'd focus on Tabitha. Not that he needed encouragement. He resisted the urge to brush her soft, blonde hair from her brow and ease her frown.

She blinked and turned toward the bag he'd dropped on the fake-marble counter earlier when she needed to open her potion. While she rummaged inside, she said, "My manners are appalling. Would you like something to drink? Beer? Wine?"

"Water is fine." Not that either of the other options she'd presented would render him remotely inebriated. Ale and wine here paled in comparison to the deep, rich flavors he preferred from Lanorinian libations.

She put the paper-wrapped, giant burrito on the plate she'd removed from the overhead cabinet, then opened another to pull a tall glass from within. An efficient pivot and she opened one side of the golden yellow refrigerator for ice. Then she accessed the other side and removed a water pitcher from within.

While she poured, she said, "The well water is a bit hard."

When she replaced the container, he noticed she had little food inside—eggs, a couple of apples in a plastic bag, some small yogurt containers, the water, and a tin of coffee. He'd thought her request to stop at the burrito place strange, but if her refrigerator held this little food, the stop made sense.

She filled the glass to the top with water and handed the drink to him, then his plate. His stomach rumbled, eager for sustenance. Somehow, he suppressed a wince at the embarrassing sound.

With a small, amused smile, she led him into another room, to a table with one placemat, which she neatly swapped to the long side. With a sweep of her hand, she indicated he should sit where she'd placed the floral, cork-backed mat. She retrieved another from the sideboard and placed it in front of her, then set her takeout bowl atop.

With a negligent wave, she said, "Please, sit. I forgot silverware."

His upbringing declared he would wait until she returned. While out of eyesight, he monitored her movements with his sharp hearing. The itch still hadn't abated.

Within moments, she returned with the forks and knives, and she gazed to him with puzzlement. "You can sit, you know."

"I was waiting for you."

She stilled and stared at him like an exotic species. In a flurry of movement, she handed him silverware and headed to her seat. "I haven't had company in a while. Thank you."

He followed her and while he helped scoot her chair in, he said, "You're welcome." Once he'd taken his seat, he unwrapped the burrito's end. Eschewing the utensils, he ate in silence for several bites, which for him meant half the spicy meal. She picked at her food and remained silent as well.

His instinct still bugged him. "Why don't you have a ward system here when most paranormals seem to have them?"

With her lengthy pause, he chastised himself for a lack of social skills. But she could use the magical protection way out in the country where anyone or anything could be lurking. He snuck a glance to the large picture window, but the chandelier's glow made the glass into a virtual one-way mirror.

Finally, she said, "Grandma was a regular human, and though she lived outside Split, she never knew about the paranormal world. When I got her property, I didn't really need wards. An empath working in a human advertising company isn't exactly someone criminals like the Underground would want."

The last sentence rankled. Lord Regus Roundtree, one of the leaders within the insidious criminal gang, might be in the North American Council's Chinati maximum security prison for his crimes. But he'd sworn vengeance against anyone involved with his son, like Thelma who had helped with the wedding. She owned Boutique Magique, which employed Tabitha. Convoluted and tangential to Tabby? Yes. And exactly the way Lord Regus would think. From his barred cell, he'd take any opportunity to lash out against even the most peripherally involved.

Rather than scare her with his knowledge of the twisted fae's reasoning, Fernald said, "You're far outside town with little protection. I'm pretty sure you could get a deal from Vargas Security Systems."

Tabitha pushed some of her food to the side of her bowl, then put down her fork. She opened her mouth, then pain flashed across her face. "I'll look into it."

The MendMe must not be working as quickly as she hoped. He wished he could soothe the slight frown from her brow. "Did you want to go lie down?"

For a moment, she appeared confused. "Oh, no. My head is quite a bit better. I just…" She pulled her napkin from her lap and folded the paper until it returned to its original square. Whatever she wanted or didn't want to say seemed to be important. He remained silent.

After she put the serviette on the table next to her plate, she said, "Ward systems are expensive when you can't do them yourself." Her brittle smile turned brave. "But I'm hoping that will change. I've got three interviews lined up in the next two days. If all goes well, I'll have a new job, with a new salary and the ability to get a basic ward package soon."

Hell. “I spoke without thinking. You mentioned your husband had—”

“Ex.” She’d practically shouted the word, which seemed to echo in the quiet house. She fiddled with one of the napkin’s corners before saying in a more moderate tone, “Ex-husband. Archer and I have been divorced for almost two years.”

If he didn’t stop shoving his feet in his mouth he’d surely choke on them soon. “My apologies.”

She expelled a huge breath. “I need to stop being so snippy. Half the damn population is divorced, and a lot of those multiple times. I won’t be the last to be betrayed by someone they loved, right?”

“Certainly not. Those who can hurt you the worst are often the closest to you.” Witness his father. And most of his brothers. He took a big bite of the burrito to ensure he didn’t say more.

“You sound as if—” A long-haired, tortoiseshell cat leapt up to the table opposite of Tabitha.

Must be a good hunter. He hadn’t heard a sound. The cat ignored him and stared at Tabby with bright copper eyes.

“Clio. Get down. We have company.” She rose and started toward the feline, who sat with what appeared to be expectation.

He swallowed his mouthful. “She’s fine.”

“You sure? I rarely have guests, and she’s gotten used to eating dinner with me.”

He glanced at Clio, who took him in with cool interest. “I like cats. Besides, not my house.”

“Thank you.” She opened a drawer on a sideboard next to the table and took out a tiny can of food and a small white bowl. “Do you mind? Some people don’t think it’s the best smelling stuff.”

“Not at all.” Between her acid tone, the fact she had few

visitors, and mentioning that she ate with the cat each night, Fernald concluded Archer had been the one who didn't like the smell.

She popped the lid and dumped the contents into the bowl. While the odor didn't entice Fernald, he'd smelled far worse in Lord Regus's dungeons.

While her cat attacked her meal with a delicate gusto, Tabitha retook her seat. He finished off the last bite of his burrito then narrowed his gaze on her own meal, concerned. "You haven't eaten anything."

"I'm not really hungry. I didn't eat any, if you'd like it." She gave the takeout bowl a gentle push toward him.

Though it would've sated a normal man, the oversized burrito merely took the sharp edge from his hunger. Gargoyles had immense appetites. Her offer tempted him, but by the state of her refrigerator, he suspected she'd need the meal tomorrow.

He balled up his meal's wrapping, added his napkin, then rose. "Thanks, but the burrito was perfect. I think I'll be on my way. You sure you don't want someone to come and stay with you tonight? I heard your head hit the rock. Seemed pretty bad."

"I hope I didn't rush you. I'm fine, though, by myself."

Had there been a hint of wistfulness in her tone? Best not to overstay his welcome, and right now, the temptation to remain rode him too hard. He put his plate and water glass in the sink, then turned. A bump against his leg stilled him, and he glanced down to where Clio rubbed her forehead and cheek against his shin. Her purr could've been mistaken for a lion's. His heart squeezed with the cat's affection.

"Wow." Tabitha's mouth hung in an "O" before she snapped her lips shut. "She doesn't usually like people."

Clio sat and stared at him, something akin to expectation in her wide, golden eyes.

He bent down and rubbed the side of his finger against her cheek, then under her chin. The cat leaned into the attention, closing her eyes and jutting out her jaw. So soft.

"I don't know if I…" Tabitha's words trailed off when the purring kicked into high overdrive. "Well then. She normally takes a swipe at people who get that close. I guess she really *does* like you."

"I had a kitten when I was younger." A fluffy white fur ball flashed into his memory with a spasm of his heart. He straightened, stepped over Clio, and headed toward the door before he betrayed himself.

"Good night," he said instead of revealing his father killed Starlight so no one would mistake his progeny as "soft."

Fernald shut the door on her murmured farewell. His father's brutal lesson taught him to never put another at risk by showing his emotions. And he'd almost slipped.

He stepped out into the night and shifted into his gargoyle form, the one his father praised as the pinnacle of the gargoyle breeding program. The itch hadn't left. Time to go on patrol. His clothing changed with him, accommodating the wings that burst from his back, as well as fitting to his bulk and increased height. He had the preternatural speed of a demon, strength of a bear shifter, skin nearly as impervious as dragon hide, and senses more tuned than a wolf-shifter. The perfect fighting machine.

Time he acted like the weapon he'd been bred to be.

CHAPTER 5

When it became apparent Clio would knead enough biscuits to feed an army, Tabby cracked her lids. The cat's purr accelerated, and her claws pricked through the sheet and Tabby's T-shirt. "Ow, you. I'm awake."

Only once she'd given Clio the scritches she desired did the cat rise from her loafed position on Tabby's chest. Tail held high and twitching at the end, her spiraling prance across the coverlet signaled she wanted her meal.

Tabby flicked her gaze to the clock on the nightstand. Oh boy. Ten-thirty, an hour that accounted for the bright light filtering around the blinds. Huh. Rarely did she get to sleep in like this, and her laziness felt amazing. Best to get moving, though she still had a couple hours until her first interview. Of the three, she wanted this position the most. She went over a list of pre-interview priorities—one last review of the agency's bigger clients and their current campaigns, as well as a pep talk to get her ready for the questions about her ex's allegations.

Ugh. She scrubbed a hand over her face. Mercifully, the headache she'd had after last night's meeting with Enchanted

Rock's granite had dissipated. The MendMe had largely done its job, which included leaving her mouth an arid wasteland.

A demanding "meow" called from the end of her bed, and she slipped from between the covers. She still had a hard time believing her notoriously people-hating cat cozied up to Fernald that way. The empathy and sorrow she'd felt coming from him when he bent to pet Clio nearly overwhelmed Tabby. As had the swift eradication of the feeling as if excised by a scalpel. What could've caused that—

Her phone rang from its place on the nightstand. A selfie picture of Tabby and her best friend, Yvette Prada, showed on the screen. Both she and Tabby wore last year's Halloween costumes. Yvette had won the Best Ironic Costume category in Mingo's contest by taking a good likeness of a comic book antihero to laugh-out-loud ironic since the petite brunette was an actual wolverine shifter. Tabby had dressed as an Orion female from the original Star Trek series, with sixties winged eyeliner plus green skin and dark brown hair. Both she and Yvette had posed with crossed eyes and tongues stuck out. The caller ID pic always made Tabby smile.

She tapped the green button and started across the house to put some kibble into Clio's bowl. "Hey, Yvette."

"Where are you? You coming into work today?" The lack of a greeting was unusual, as was her friend's neutral, but serious, tone.

"I have some interviews this morning, and I hadn't planned to go in. Why?"

"Aw hell." Yvette huffed. "I'm glad to hear you're getting back to applying for jobs. I still have that shovel if you have need to bury a certain body."

Yvette was Tabby's ride or die. Even if she knew the wolverine shifter joked about helping bury Archer in an unmarked grave, she'd been the best friend someone in the middle of divorcing a narcissist could have. Her friend had also recently been promoted to investigator within North American Council Security, probably for her tenacity at both solving cases and following the rules.

Tabby huffed a laugh. "Thanks for the offer, but I think your employer would frown on murder. Besides, I don't think burying my ex in a shallow grave is why you're calling."

"No," Yvette said, her voice returning to a clipped precision. "Someone broke into First Bank of Enchanted Rock last evening."

Whoa. The premiere paranormal bank prided itself on its security measures. She'd arrived at the sideboard where she kept Clio's kibble and sandwiched the phone between her ear and shoulder to pull out the box. "The bank's wards got them, right?"

"Nope."

Tabby flipped the top and began to pour the pellets into the cat's bowl. "Uh oh. But why are you calling me?"

"We think the same person ran into you while escaping with the goods."

Holy cow. She put the bowl at the end of the table where Clio ate. "The guy who mowed me down robbed the bank? What did he take?"

"Burglarized the bank since they were closed, but yeah, that guy. We reviewed the video from all the cameras we could, but he was exceptionally good at diverting his face. Tall, muscular, brown hair, dark clothing. That's all I got. I need you to help us make a sketch of what he looked like."

"I didn't even see his face." The back of her head throbbed a little while Tabby re-ran the memory to confirm her statement, though she knew she hadn't gotten a look at his features.

Yvette had an extremely colorful swear word repertoire,

and she put them to use in creative ways that made Tabby smile despite the topic's seriousness. Her friend tacked on a sigh at the end. "Okay. Did you see anything before that? Boutique Magique faces the side of the building where they gained entry."

"No—wait. I did see something right after I let Lauren out the door." While she made her coffee, Tabby described the shadows she'd seen flicker under the bank's eaves. "But I—"

Guilt pricked at her. She'd almost said she thought the being to be Fernald. With his former lord in prison, he might have come under scrutiny for the theft. Kidnapping. Extortion. Now possibly bank theft? No crime wasn't worth the Underground's time. Or at least that would be the logo she'd apply to the crime syndicate.

"You what?" Yvette prompted when Tabby didn't volunteer more information.

She cleared her throat. "I saw a flicker of shadows, but I didn't see who or what."

For this round of expletives, Yvette kept her language relatively mild. "I am not catching a break here."

"I know. I wish I had a lead for you." Tabby winced. Not exactly how someone should treat their ride or die.

"Okay. Who helped you up?"

Whew. She'd bought Tabby's fib. "Fernald Grayson, Mouse's half-brother. He asked Fernald to keep an eye on the shop while he's out of town on business."

"Why?"

"With the way Thelma helped Brie and Xavier with the wedding dress, Mouse thought Regus might make good on his threat to harm whoever helped them get married. Fernald's been skulking around the shop now for a couple of days."

"Skulking?"

The word implied negativity, and even before Tabby found

out about the burglary, she was grateful to him for his help last night. Her cheeks warmed, and she shut the cabinet door a little harder than she intended. "Yeah, mainly sitting outside the tea shop on the far corner where he can see the front door."

"You have any reason to believe he might be involved?"

Tabby almost laughed at the hopefulness in her friend's voice. "None. But I don't know him all that well. Just that my head hurt badly enough that he brought me home, and he's a heck of a driver."

"Why do you say that?"

"Some jerk in an SUV nearly ran us over on the way home." A restless energy moved her to the other end of the dining table and the window that looked out over the front of the yard. Light streamed in, and she pushed apart the drapes.

"You let him drive you home? Why didn't you call me?"

The combo of suspicion and hurt in Yvette's voice tugged at Tabby's heart. "Because it would've taken at least an hour and a half for you to come get me, nag at me to see a medic, get me to my house, then go back to yours. He was right there."

Despite better sense earned from a nasty divorce saying Tabby should be suspicious of any male, her gut said he meant her no harm. "Besides, he's begun working for Hebert Security. I doubt they would use him if they didn't trust him—he's not even a shifter and they seem to think he's okay. I've met him several times, and I haven't gotten any weird vibes from him. And before you tell me that I've been fooled in the past, that's why I texted Thelma that he took me home. And I knew the cameras inside the Rock would see me leave with someone."

Despite the abrupt manner of his departure, he'd been polite and respectful. And genuinely concerned.

"Good points. But I still worry about you."

"I appreciate it." Tabby meant every word. "Not everyone has a NACS officer watching over them."

"And not everyone has a great friend like you. I have to run. If you think of anything, let me know."

While she said her goodbye, Tabby pushed aside the sheer curtains to let more light in, something she hadn't done in a while since she'd been working at the boutique as much as she could. The day shone sunny and clear. Perhaps after she got done with her interviews, she could weed in one of the planting beds…

Wait. For several moments she couldn't believe what faced her. She moved to the front door, threw the ornately carved dark wood wide, and charged outside to the small stoop.

From her vantage point three steps above grade, she took in the yard that had been fenced off from the rest of the acreage. Not a thistle, not a stem of henbit, not a blade of crabgrass, not a bit of any other weed marred the planting bed, infested the grass, or stuck out their leaves from the chinks in the concrete walkway. The shrubs against the house were trimmed neatly, but in an organically pleasing way, with all evidence of the invasive, climbing bindweed erased.

What…? How…?

Around the corner of the house came whistling, and she turned to find a figure carrying a coiled hose. His black cargo pants were smudged at the knees and his hands darkened with dirt.

Fernald.

CHAPTER 6

While Fernald whistled an old fae tune, he looped the last bit of hose in his hand and congratulated himself on a job well-done, despite the challenges of finding the implements in the barn out back.

Last night, he'd grown bored with simply watching and waiting for whoever stalked Tabby. One thistle became fifty. Pulling the grass from the beds became mowing. Taking a small tree's branch from scraping the side of the house became pruning the bushes and pulling bindweed.

Now all Tabby would have to do would be put some mulch on the beds and trim some of the trees back from the house. He could accomplish only so much in one night and most of the morning. Opening his hearing abilities to their maximum limit, he sought indications Tabitha had awakened. He'd been at the barn for far too long.

"Fernald?"

He stopped whistling and turned his focus to Tabitha, who stood outside her front door on a small concrete pad, clad only in a T-shirt and yoga pants. With mussed hair, she might have just risen from her bed. For a moment, his heart lurched with longing, then he took in her curious expression, somewhere between fury and disbelief. Shit. He thought he'd been quiet while he worked.

"Glad to see you're up. I apologize if I woke you." He crossed to the walkway leading to the front door. "If you hadn't stirred soon, I was going to call you."

Confusion flitted across her features. "Why?"

"Thought you'd be okay after taking the MendMe, but I wanted to make sure the concussion hadn't done more harm. Slow brain leak, whatever." He stopped at the base of the stairs. "Didn't want to pound on your door and scare you."

"No. I mean, thanks, but I meant why—how—did you do all this?" Her hand swept out toward the yard.

"How? I had all night and some of the morning. Why?" Discomfort trickled into his stomach. "You said your gardener had quit on you, and I thought I could help."

"You're a lawn guy?" The suspicion in her tone pricked his pride.

"No, well, I enjoy gardening in my spare time." Now why'd he tell her that? He'd hidden the love for plants deep. *Relax*. She couldn't take his hobby from him.

Her mouth hung open, her arms remained spread wide, and her silence grew.

Had he offended her? Hell. "I just thought…well…" His gaze swept to the perfectly shaped plantings and immaculate beds. "Maybe it was a bit much."

She put her arms down. "Um, while I'm grateful, I don't quite know what to say."

He let out his pent-up breath carefully through his nose. "What else beyond gratitude *is* there to say?"

She squinted and stared at him with a side-eye. "You don't want *anything* else?"

"No. Why?"

"Not a date?"

Her suspicious tone began to grate. Then he remembered her ex. He must've been a real asshole. Fernald reconsidered his prior evening's position on violence to the man. "I do find you attractive, but I didn't do this to guilt you into going to dinner with me."

She put her hands on her hips and gave him a look that said she might've been trying to pierce his fragile mental defenses. "Huh."

He'd said nothing but the truth. "What?"

"Nothing."

He remained silent, since he had nothing further to offer by way of explanation.

"Fine. This feels like love bombing, and I'm freaking out a little." She crossed her arms and hunched her shoulders.

"Love bombing?" Whatever the term meant couldn't be good.

She took in a careful breath as if she steeled herself for his response, then said, "A non-technical term for when someone uses over-the-top gifts in an effort to manipulate the other person. Archer did it all the time at the outset of our relationship, and all this is…well, I…"

During her explanation, anger grew within Fernald. Why would she think so little of him that she would compare him to her ex? He struck that asshole off the "maybe" list for retribution and put him firmly on the "to-do" list. When he spotted the haunted expression in her eyes, any annoyance dissipated. "Look. I do find you attractive. I've already said that. But I do like gardening. Yours was a bit overgrown. I overstepped my bounds. I apologize."

Something brushed against his leg, and he glanced down to find Clio winding between his feet. She began to purr and stared at him with expectation. Despite a klaxon blaring in his head, he bent down to pet her.

"Clio—you know you aren't allowed outside." Tabitha hustled down the steps and scooped the feline into her arms, then shot him an unfathomable glance which might've carried a hint of apology. "I'm going to make some breakfast. Would you like some eggs and bacon?"

His stomach rumbled, and he shot her a rueful grin. "I think that's a yes."

Clio hissed, and his gaze darted to the feline.

"Ow, hey!" Tabitha dropped her cat and brought her finger to her mouth, sucking on it. What could have caused her pet to do that? The cat had seemed calm a minute earlier, even after Tabitha picked her up. Now, Clio stood facing toward the yard, back arched, tail straight up, while she hissed several more times. Then the feline scampered into the house.

"Cat, I swear…" Tabitha muttered. She shook her head as if to clear her thoughts then turned to him. "Come on. I've got a bit before I need to get ready for my interview, and I'm hungry."

For a moment, he hesitated, trying to sense through smell or hearing what might've angered the cat. Nothing. He followed her inside, and she not only shut the door behind him but also applied the deadbolt. Good. Out in the middle of nowhere like this, she should keep herself secure at all times.

Once in the kitchen, she bent at the waist to a lower cabinet. "How do you like your eggs?"

"Yes."

She glanced over her shoulder back to him. "I'm sorry?"

She probably had no idea how wildly his body reacted at this moment—his pulse kicked up, lungs seized. He cleared his throat, silently berating himself for allowing his control to slip.

"Any way you want to fix them. I don't discriminate, especially when someone else is doing the cooking."

"Over easy then." Her low laughter while she pulled a pan from below only added to the dismay caused by his rampaging arousal.

Desperate for any reason to distract himself, he said, "I need to wash my hands."

"Through the den, down the hall, first door on the left." She hadn't glanced at him while she laid out the bacon and turned on the burner. Good. Hopefully she hadn't heard the strain in his voice.

He hurried down to the bathroom and took his time getting the grime out from under each nail. Finally his breathing slowed to normal, and his heart wasn't ready to explode from his chest. Agreeing to breakfast may not have been the smartest idea, but he'd felt bad and didn't want to reject her kindness.

He froze. *Stop lying to yourself. You want to spend more time with her.*

Back at the kitchen, he found silverware on the peninsula, and he took the hint to set the table. Clio lounged on her end of the gleaming wood, her purr practically a truck's engine, then she rolled over.

Instead of taking the invitation, he mechanically began to place the flatware and napkins. By the time he'd finished, he'd remembered why he didn't want anything that could be taken from him.

Tabby was not that different from the kitten, at least in gargoyle terms. Delicate and beautiful.

Easily harmed.

When he returned to the kitchen, the bacon already sizzled in the skillet, a delicious aroma.

Her gaze cut to him from the corner of her eye, then back to her task. "Um, you like gardening?"

Safer topic.

"At first, I thought I'd just pull the thistles. Don't need gloves for that." He held up his hands, gratified when she huffed a laugh. "Then the rest of the weeds seemed to stand out and had to go too. The shrubs needed some pruning. Then the grass seemed a bit long." He rubbed the back of his neck, where heat had gathered. "I can see where you'd think I'd be going over the top."

"How'd you mow the grass?"

"I found an old reel mower in the barn, and I needed a little oil to free up the gears. Found a file for the blade too."

The spatula she'd used to take the bacon from the pan halted in midair, and her shoulders tensed. Her voice took on a tone curiously devoid of emotion when she said, "You went into the barn."

Not again. No matter what he did he seemed to do something wrong. "I think I need to apologize again. Or should I go?"

"No," she said hurriedly, then whipped around to face him, her cheeks glazed with pink. "No. I'm embarrassed. Grandma hoarded a little. And while I've gotten most of the house done, I haven't had time to clean out the barn yet."

That probably accounted for the house's stale smell he'd detected the prior day. He glanced around trying to picture the piles of stuff he'd seen in the barn stacked haphazardly around him, everything from empty fifty-gallon drums to old aluminum lawn chairs missing their webbing to dusty boxes of old magazines. Wherever he looked in the house, he couldn't see a speck of dirt.

"If this place was as packed as the barn, then you should be proud of yourself. That's a big job ahead of you. But she has some great tools. They don't make them like that anymore."

She added a slight head tilt to her wrinkled brow before she turned back to her skillet. Four cracks later, eggs sizzled in the pan. "It was hard. I'm still not done with the house."

"Really? I never would've guessed your grandmother had a problem." He glanced around once more. Nothing out of place. Impressive.

"Thanks." Some of the tension seemed to drain from her shoulders, and she started shuttling eggs to plates. "But I haven't tackled Grandma's room yet."

The sadness in her voice caught his attention. "Overwhelming amount or too many memories or both?"

"Both." After the clipped word, she handed him a plate containing three fried eggs, then also a plate with several pieces of toast, which he took with him to the table.

"Thanks. I don't often get a homemade meal." Before she could respond, he continued, "I understand how dealing with her room could be that way. A friend left me something after they passed, and I haven't opened it yet." The battered box with its beautiful gold name plaque sat in the bottom of his empty duffle, the only possession he kept from Lanorinia, one he prayed no one would ever find or recognize.

"Really? I'd probably die of curiosity."

Curiosity? The idea of opening Linden's gift gave him both pain and a sense of betrayal for not having done so for thirty years.

"What are you thinking?" she asked softly.

"Bad memory."

She reached out and briefly covered his hand with hers before withdrawing. "I'm sorry if I brought up something from Lord Regus."

The comfort and empathy she gave filled his heart with

warmth. He'd never told anyone about his childhood's cold brutality, largely because when growing up, every other gargoyle family seemed to be the same. Certainly no one in the fae realm, or here on Earth for that matter, cared how gargoyles were treated by their elf masters. Once Xavier released his father's indentured gargoyles, Fernald figured no one wanted to hear about his childhood. Everyone had their struggles, like Tabitha and her ex-husband.

He cleared his throat. "It wasn't Lord Regus."

She forked a bite of egg and chewed, speculation in her gaze. She must've thought better of questioning, and he appreciated her discretion. But hadn't she been forthcoming with her troubles? How could she use his pain for ill? She had no control over him.

"When I was younger, my father told me to not hang around the gardener, a brownie named Linden, on Lord Regus's estate. Father didn't use physical punishment. He preferred to take away things that I cared for. Rather than him harming Linden, I stayed away."

"You're built for one thing—death and destruction, and a soft gargoyle's not worth the air they breathe." His father's brutality still chilled Fernald to the core.

He shook himself free of the echoing memory. "Years later, Linden passed to fly with the gods and a box came to me from him."

"You'll know when the time is right."

The small encouraging smile she offered him lifted him from the cold memories. Perhaps she had a point. "Thank you. You will also with your grandmother's room."

Never had he been accused of lacking courage, though around Tabitha he felt like he did nothing but fumble. Yet opening up to her felt right in his heart. He should ask her out now. "Would you like to have—"

Tabitha jabbed her finger toward the kitchen. “Fire!”

CHAPTER 7

The barn stood about fifty yards behind the house, visible through a window over the sink. With frozen horror, she observed choking clouds of smoke pouring from inside.

Fernald had already leapt from his seat and scrambled out the front door before Tabby had even gained her feet. Why would he travel the opposite direction?

Instead of following him, she raced to the kitchen to grab her phone from the counter, then headed to the den and slipped outside. She made sure to close the sliding door. She didn't need Clio getting spooked and running off.

She kept going across the cracked concrete patio, small rocks jabbing into her bare feet, but she couldn't stop. Everything she had could go up in flames if the fire spread to the dry grass and brush, then her home.

Fernald sprinted past her, coiled hose in hand. She dashed after him, trying desperately to unlock her phone to call 9-1-1, but she fumbled several times when sharp stabs to her feet made her stumble. Dimly she recognized the needle-like pain as sticker-burrs. Though she wanted to stop and pull the evil burrs from her feet, she had to save her property.

She reached the barn, the soles of her feet burning with agony. Finally, she forced her shaking fingers to unlock the device, and she pressed the screen's buttons until she reached the number pad to dial. Fernald stood inside the large door's opening, next to a barrel with a running hose, yet did nothing while the water spattered onto the dirt floor.

Why didn't he spray? Hold on. The breeze shifted direction and revealed the threat came from a fifty-gallon drum on one side of the narrow pathway. No flames showed at the top, but copious amounts of smoke billowed forth.

"Were you burning the weeds? Why didn't you take the barrel outside? You could've burned down the whole damn barn. Even the house." Fury blazed and her voice rose until she screeched at him like a banshee. How dare he?

He didn't respond. Instead, his wings sprouted from his back. His arms and legs lengthened. He grabbed the barrel and pulled the drum backward.

She leapt out of the way just in time to avoid him knocking her to the sandy ground with a sweep of his wing. By the time she straightened, he'd stuffed the still-running hose into the makeshift fire pit, which he'd tugged several yards from the barn.

Swear words as vicious as Yvette's fell from Tabby's lips. He'd put everything she owned at risk. She hobbled over to him, betrayal fueling the inferno within her. "You should've done that in the first place."

He pivoted toward her, and his fangs had descended over his lower lip, brow heavier, cheekbones chiseled. Against his gray-granite-hued skin his eyes glowed a bright teal. "This was a diversion." His voice had lowered to a gruff rumble, and she struggled to hear him over the ragged pounding of her heart. With urgency, he tugged on her arm. "Come on."

She shook free his hand and dug in her heels. "What are you talking about? Did you say a diversion?"

"I didn't put the weeds in the barrel, much less light them on fire." He glanced over his shoulder toward the house.

"What?"

"I didn't do that." He pointed to the barrel which now had only a thin trickle of smoke rising from the top.

"Then who did?"

"I don't know. But something is going on here. We need to get back to the house."

"The house?" Her heart kicked into double time despite her confusion.

His motions a blur, he picked her up and slung her over his shoulder. She'd barely had time for an, "Oof!" when her stomach met his rock-hard shoulder and then his wing covered over her head.

"Hey—"

"Shh," he said quietly, and put her down to the side of the sliding door.

Pain burned the soles of her feet and evaporated her stinging putdown. Immediately she rolled her arches up and out until she stood on the sides of her soles, then lifted one to start pulling at the stickers. Tears pushed to her lids, and she sucked in a breath with a whimper.

Grimacing as if he shared the pain with her, he whispered, "Sorry about that. Did you leave the sliding door open?"

She glanced up, and the burning agony receded replaced by a cold trickle snaking down her spine. Clio. After a swallow to wet her dry mouth, she whispered back, "No."

If possible, his features hardened further. In the slightest murmur, he said, "Can't leave you alone. Going over my shoulder."

Even if she'd protested the method, he probably would've

ignored her. Besides, did she really want to be left alone with whoever was inside, even if merely a mortal? No.

Fernald handled her more gently this time. His leathery wing lifted, then covered her, pressing into her head and back. More pressure across her butt and curling around her thighs didn't feel like a hand. He must have used the claw at his wing's top end to hold her in place.

After she tensed her abdominals for whatever jolting journey ensued, she turned her face to the side so her nose and lips weren't forced against him. A gargoyle's granite skin wasn't exactly forgiving. A hint of daylight filtered through his leathery wing, but otherwise, she was blind to the events around her and completely at his mercy.

For a millisecond, panic gripped her when she recognized the vulnerable position she'd placed herself in. *Relax. He could've attacked you when he brought you home last night.*

He started to move silently. Though he didn't jostle her like before, she could sense his direction. Into the den, then the dining area. Down the hallway. Quick, efficient. She strained her senses to hear anything beyond the low, steady thump of his heart under her ear.

A hiss and feral moan sounded an awful lot like Clio. Tabby smothered a cry of relief.

His shoulder rocked, and she jerked when he lunged forward. For her cat? He stumbled and pivoted, then regained his balance. Never once did his wing lose its grasp on her. Nor did she hear Clio protest again.

He lunged once more and what sounded like a man cried out. Her blood turned cold. *Someone broke into her house.* She brought her hand to her mouth to stifle her sobs.

"Reveal yourself intruder." The gargoyle's raspy voice carried no hint of fear.

Rapid footsteps. With another hiss from Clio, Fernald

moved again, now pounding back down the hallway at his preternatural speed. Maybe to the front door? He stopped. A click, then his pivot made her dizzy. He didn't move for several moments, allowing her to regain her balance. She strained her hearing for anything, but all she could discern were the wild beats of her own heart and her ragged breaths.

He started forward, stealthily once more. She'd lost all sense of direction, and her ribs began to ache with the pressure. A rolling sound came to her ears. The sliding door?

A savage muttered word she didn't understand came from Fernald a moment before he released his wing's grip and shifted her cradle-like into his arms.

She wrapped her hands around his nape, gasping with the release of her body's pressure on her abdomen, vaguely aware what she'd just heard—he'd closed the sliding glass door.

A grimace covered his feature's harsh planes, making the expression all that more savage by his shifted features. Then his brow smoothed, and he turned to her with a smile that revealed the entirety of his thick, white fangs. "You okay?"

Many might've been frightened by his ferocious appearance. Instead she wondered at how protected she felt. She took a moment to take inventory of both her body and the room. Her feet? Burning with pain. Her house? From what she could view, fine. "Other than those damn sticker burrs in my feet and my ribs being a bit abused from your shoulder, I'm okay. You want to tell me what just happened?"

He put her on the couch, then sat at the far end and put her feet in his lap. "The burn pit had wet grass piled about halfway up—it accounts for the smoke and said whoever started the fire didn't want to burn down the barn, just get you—and probably me—out of the house."

She hissed when he plucked out one of the burrs and held up the pea-sized, devilish seedpod. "Those are brutal. I'll get the rest. When I got back inside, I saw someone had dumped your purse on the counter."

Her gaze darted to the kitchen, but she couldn't see beyond the peninsula from her position. Anger and confusion mixed into a ball that bounced around in her brain. "My purse? Did they steal my wallet?"

He paused his ministrations. "I don't know. There was quite a pile. Do you want me to look?"

"Could you?" The sting in her soles might as well have been a thousand needles.

He gently placed her feet to the side, rose, and crossed to the kitchen. He moved a couple of things, then held up her black, trifold wallet, much to her relief.

"That's it."

He brought the item to her, and while she flipped through the contents, he resumed removing the embedded spines. Cards. Cash. Driver's license. Picture of her parents taken a couple days before they died in a car wreck. All were there. She refolded and snapped the wallet closed while trying to order what he'd told her. Nothing made sense. "You saw my purse…what happened then?"

"I didn't see anyone but heard Clio hiss, similar to what she did outside, which confused me then but not now. Sorry," he said when his claws dug a little hard after one of the burr spines that remained in her foot, and she took in a swift breath. His sympathetic gaze flashed to hers. "This one's a little deep."

"No, please continue." The dexterity he had with his claws impressed her, but she steeled herself against making further noises because she would have a hard time doing this herself. Causing pain even to remove a splinter from her own finger often became an ordeal, and don't get her started on her own blood. Much to her shame, she'd passed out, hit her head, and got stitches when she saw a cut her grandma had that bled profusely.

He bent back to his task. "I followed Clio's hiss to one of the bedrooms—yours, I think. Your belongings were everywhere, the cat was arched and facing nothing. At least nothing I could see."

She held back a yelp, but he must've felt her flinch because he stopped. "Sorry. I can take you to the med ward if you like."

The idea of having a tech spend time pulling something as insignificant as burr spines from her feet, no matter how much they hurt her, made little sense when she had someone whose claws seemed as good as tweezers. "Keep going and don't mind my jumps. I'll say something if it hurts a lot. You're actually quite gentle."

The juxtaposition of his grin with his fierce features made him almost handsome. Concentration brought creases to the corner of his eyes when he refocused his attention. "Okay. I couldn't see what caused your cat to react. I assumed someone had an invisibility cloak or spell. I tried to grab them, but the male—sounded like a male—evaded my grasp. I figured he'd try to escape, and I was right, just guessed wrong at the exit point. He used the front door as a diversion, I suspect, and exited out the back."

The self-castigation in Fernald's tone made her want to set him at ease because he'd put two and two together while she hadn't even recognized the numbers yet, let alone come to understand what the answer meant. "If he was invisible, then you wouldn't know his position."

"I listened but couldn't hear him any longer. I could've chased, maybe even taken wing to try to follow, but that would've left you alone. I'm going to call Mouse in a minute.

We may have a problem with Lord Regus." The tone in Fernald's voice turned grim.

A quiver rocked the meager bites of egg she'd eaten earlier at the thought of the evil fae targeting her. Something nagged at the periphery of her thoughts. Her phone call from the morning. "Before you do that, we may have a different problem."

While Tabitha recounted her phone call with her friend from North American Council Security, a muscle started to jump in his cheek, and his dark scowl might've frightened her. Instead, the prospect she'd been caught in the crosshairs of a diabolical plot terrified her.

"He might think I can identify him. Why not come after me directly? Why would they search my purse? Come invisibly? I'm only an HP. They know where I live if they want to hurt or threaten me." Even kill her. Bitter bile rose in her throat.

He remained silent for several moments, staring into the distance. She would've broken the silence, except he had much more experience in this type of situation. His intense electric-blue gaze connected with hers. "He could've slipped something into your purse."

A punch to her solar plexus couldn't have more effectively robbed her of breath. The idea hadn't occurred to her. "He helped me up, then handed me my bag. Oh shit."

Each word had her convinced Fernald had come the correct conclusion. "But what could it have been? I didn't take anything from my purse last night when I came home, and he dumped my bag out first, because you found him in my bedroom, right?"

"Hmm. That *is* strange. Let's see if you notice anything he missed." He put her feet to the side, rose, and crossed to the kitchen. Shortly, he brought back the large tote, the bag acting as a plate for what it should've contained.

While he seated himself and resumed pulling the burrs from her soles, she searched through the items she kept within. Random receipts, a daily planner still bound with its elastic, small makeup bag, brush, and a myriad of other things she recognized. Geez. Maybe she needed to weed out some of this stuff. No wonder the dang thing felt extra heavy last night.

Next she poked around in the interior and the large pocket where she stored her most used items—phone, keys, and her favorite lip gloss. Nothing remained inside.

"I don't see anything missing, except for my phone, but I think I dropped that outside at the barn." Frustration with a lack of answers bristled inside her and she wanted to throw the bag across the room. Instead, she curled her fingers into the leather and squeezed as hard as she could.

"You were probably a bit preoccupied with the effects of hitting your head. I should've paid more attention."

His tone had been bleak, and she could feel the anger he directed at himself. When had she turned on her empathic senses? Habit since… She uncurled her fingers and reached toward him, grazing his bicep. "Really—not your fault. You couldn't have known."

Denial emanated from him like a wave. Before she could reassure him again, he said, "What I can do is make sure you're not in danger again. I think we need to talk to your friend at NACS."

CHAPTER 8

Tabitha tipped her head back against the couch's pillow and groaned. "That's all I need. Stuck in an interview room all day—my interview." A stricken expression crossed her features, and she sat up abruptly. Her tote and the contents slid to the floor with thumps against the carpet.

With one hand she patted her hair, the other half-covered her face, then her shoulders fell. "What time is it? Noon? I only have a half hour. Dammit. Yvette'll want me to come in immediately. This is the job I really wanted too."

After what he'd gleaned of her last couple of years, she needed this break. By the gods, he would make sure she got a chance.

"I'll call your friend if you want to get ready." He'd also call Mouse. While the bank burglar might be the culprit, the specter of Lord Regus couldn't be discounted, even from the stronghold of NAC's paranormal prison.

"Would you? Where's my phone?" She glanced around wildly and got to her feet, only to yelp and plop back down to the cushions. Her lower lip trembled.

While she'd had a shitty twenty-four hours, she couldn't

give in now. A tear began to track down her cheek and he wiped away the drop with his thumb. "You don't want red eyes or nose for your interview." He scooped her up and headed toward the hallway leading to her bedroom, determined to help make this better. "Where do you want me to drop you off?"

She sniffed and wound her arms around his neck, burying her face against his shoulder. "Bathroom."

He wanted to merely hold her and breathe in the soft scent of her hair perched in a messy bun on the top of her head. Instead, he set her butt on the olive-green countertop next to the sink sculpted to look like a shell. "I'll find your phone. You have some antiseptic in here?"

"I do." Her brave smile tugged at his heart. "I'll put it on my feet. Just find my phone if you would."

So many on Earth here seemed to rely on their mobile devices, much more than in Lanorinia. Probably because there were no signal towers in the fae realm. "Lock the bathroom door after I leave. I don't remember you having the phone when you got back to the house. I'm going to lock the door while I'm outside. I saw your keys in the pile from your purse if you don't mind me using them?"

"Please do."

"I'll be back soon." He chafed at leaving her alone for one minute with the gods-knew-who lurking.

"Fernald?"

"Yes?"

"You've been really nice and brave and…well, thanks."

He'd heard people talk about balls of emotion clogging throats, but he'd never thought the term possible until now. After a rough swallow, he managed to say, "You're welcome."

While he raced across the house, he shoved aside his emotions. *Mitigate threats now.*

Ordinarily, he would've shifted back to his more human appearance, but if he must go outside, he might have to face the unknown assailant or possibly more than one. Best to remain full gargoyle. The brush would screen him from the road and normal humans' sight.

He located the keys in the jumble on the floor and let himself out the kitchen door leading to the carport. During his egress, he carefully turned the knob's lock tab then applied the deadbolt.

The door had been open last night. Were they in possession of a key? Perhaps they used a spell or charm to unlock the door? Had they been inside the house then? His concern jumped, but he quickly discounted that idea. Most likely they waited for her to leave for work this morning. Fernald may have even stalled their plans by sticking around. Then they became desperate and used the smoke to get him and Tabitha from the house.

Regardless of the how, they'd somehow gotten access. He needed to find the phone ASAP. A sorcerer with basic skills could still be lurking and easily enter the house protected by simple locks. The flimsy, hollow-core bathroom door wouldn't last a minute even with a regular human determined to break through.

He traced the path beginning with the patio at the back of the house and kept an ear out for a grass-rustling footstep or any other indication someone hung about. Every second of delay heaped more tension on his shoulders. His need for concentration left out calling Mouse until back inside.

Finally, he spotted the phone in the dirt just inside the metal barn's open sliding door. He quickly scanned the device, but it appeared untouched. He rushed back to the house, unwilling to leave her alone for longer than absolutely necessary and determined to revisit the need for installing wards at the next available opportunity. He'd have a talk with Lilliana Vargas about supplementing a discount if necessary. No. Tabby had experienced enough deception with her husband.

Relieved to find the door secured, he let himself back into the house. Once inside, he shifted back to his human form.

He tapped on the bathroom's shoddy plywood panel. "It's Fernald. I found your phone."

The knob rattled, then she cracked the door enough for her to slide her hand through. "Thank you." Her relief became palpable. "I'll unlock it. Yvette Prada. She should be my last call." The door swung open a little more and exposed Tabitha's bare shoulder crossed by a thin, lacy strap when she passed the phone back to him. She wiggled the device when he didn't immediately accept the return.

Chiding himself for allowing a mere glimpse of smooth skin and hint of filmy undergarment to send his senses reeling, he retreated to the living area to make the call.

Prada answered after the second ring. "Hey, lady, did you remember something?"

"It's Fernald Grayson, and before you worry, she's fine."

"Then why is it you and not her speaking right now?" Suspicion simmered under her cool tone. Smart lady.

"Because she's getting ready for her job interview. Do you want a proof of life?"

The investigator ended her short pause by saying, "In a minute. What's happening?"

"We had a problem today." He described the encounter starting with the smoke and ending with him chasing the perpetrator from the house. To conclude, he added his and Tabitha's deduction regarding the bank thief slipping the stolen goods into her purse.

Prada knew her way around swear words that would've given his father a run for his money. "Wait a minute." The line went quiet for several seconds, then she said, "I can see the incident, but not the whole exchange, so it's possible. When he didn't find what he sought in her purse, he went into her bedroom thinking it might be there?"

"That's my reasoning." His irritation bubbled to the surface, and he tamped down the emotion. "What did he steal?"

"I can't release that." Her flat tone might as well have added, "Don't even try."

The information could help narrow down the suspect list, but since the investigators took a blood oath not to reveal details of their cases without authorization, he understood the denial, though the lack of cooperation angered him, nonetheless. Once more, he wrangled his emotions back into their box. He needed a cool, calm head to get Tabitha out of this predicament.

He had to keep playing nice with NACS. "Though we could be wrong, and all of this has something to do with Regus Roundtree and his wrath at Boutique Magique for helping with Xavier and Brie's wedding. Yet the purse suggests that's not the answer."

The investigator muttered something under her breath. "I don't want her at that house any longer than she has to be. Can you get her back to the Rock, or do we need to come out?"

"I can get her back." He'd make damn sure she'd get a chance at the job she wanted first. NACS might not be accommodating.

"Good. Give me your number." He rattled off the digits, then she continued. "Now put Tabby on the phone."

He crossed to the bathroom and tapped on the door. "She wants to talk to you."

The door opened, and the polished woman he'd come to

know with sleek blonde hair pulled into a low ponytail appeared still wearing her T-shirt and yoga pants. "Thanks." With a wry grimace she accepted his offering and put the phone to her ear.

He could've eavesdropped on their conversation. Instead he tuned out their words by focusing on the woman before him. Her bright tone and smile indicated ease, but the strain at the edges of her eyes gave away her brave front. Then her features relaxed and her lower lip trembled when she said, "Thanks. I'll remember that and see you soon. Here he is."

She handed the phone back to him, then slid the length of her index finger against one of her lower lids, then the other.

His gut clenched and he mouthed, "You okay?"

With a misty smile, she nodded, then brushed past him. He tracked her while she took the couple awkward steps to her room. Her screech and screamed swear word made him jump toward her door. She shot him a murderous glare over her shoulder, then threw up her hands. Muttering darkly, she entered her room and slammed the door behind her.

The intruder had left quite a mess. He put the phone back to his ear. "I'll call you when I leave."

"Good." Prada's tone turned to curiosity when she asked, "What was the screaming about?"

"I think she didn't appreciate the way the guy rearranged her room." She'd been covered by his wing the whole time and hadn't seen the full devastation.

"We'll figure out who did this," the investigator said, then signed off the call.

Not if I find him first.

He'd heard NACS investigators were notoriously protective about their cases, but this was Tabitha, not merely one of the agency's crime victims, even if Prada's personal friend. He moved to the living area where he could sit in an easy chair and still view her door, the second one on the right. He entered the investigator's number into his phone, then dialed his half-brother, who he'd grown up calling by his first name, Henry, but now called "Mouse" like the rest of the employees of the security company that employed them.

Before Mouse answered, Clio appeared at his feet, then jumped on the padded arm of the brown, fake-leather chair. Without a pause, she crossed to his lap. For a moment, he couldn't bear to touch her—the kitten his father had killed filled his memory. Almost as if he didn't control the movement, he put his hand on her and began to stroke the cat's long fur. The rumbly purrs made stopping impossible. Then something within him settled.

Mouse said, "I was just getting ready to call you. What's going on? Is Tabby okay? Thelma just told me she found a message that Tabby fell and hit her head, and you were taking her home."

"She's fine." Before his half-brother could ask any more questions, Fernald launched into a brief of the events from both the prior day and the morning. He ended with the real reason behind his call. "Could you give us an escort to the Rock? Her car is a little, uh…" His cheeks grew warm. He didn't want to be disparaging when he didn't have a vehicle at all.

"Absolutely."

"Tabitha's got a job interview in about fifteen minutes. I don't know how long she'll be in her meeting."

"Internet?"

He hadn't considered the option. Things had been moving too swiftly. "Must be. She didn't ask me to take her anywhere."

"Okay. We stayed at my place in the Rock last night since Thelma went to work early today. I'll be there in about half an hour. You know you can borrow my ride until you find one of your own. Nathan keeps a couple of company cars for us here, and Thelma has her own as well."

Fernald didn't usually like asking for help, but right now, he would acquiesce to the logical conclusion. "I'll take you up on the offer, but it will only be until I can get one of my own sometime next week."

"If it takes longer, don't worry. I know where she lives. See you in thirty."

Crap. He'd forgotten to ask. "Hey."

"Yeah?"

"Bring guns. I have a bad feeling about this."

"I'll bring two for you and enough ammo for a troop of gargoyles."

Fernald said his farewells with a sense of gratitude for Mouse—the one family member he liked to claim. He had no idea where his father and three full brothers were. The gargoyle grapevine suggested they'd hired on as muscle for the remnants of the Sunda crime family. Luckily, Fernald's father had never been able to beat the desire to do the right thing from him.

"What do you think?" Uncertainty edged Tabitha's tone.

He chastised himself for not hearing her door open. She stood at the entry to the hallway, clad in a sleek, royal blue dress. A funky gold necklace filled the V-neck perfectly. Rather than breathe out the word "Beautiful," he swallowed his emotion and said in a deadpan manner, "The slippers clash a little though."

She glanced down to the fluffy yellow Tweety Bird scuffs on her feet and chuckled, "Yeah, but they feel better when I walk, and the interview is virtual for now."

The warm smile nearly melted his insides. "You'll do great."

She took a deep breath and gave him two thumbs up. “Alright, I’m going in.”

With a careful pivot, she entered the bedroom furnished into an office, something he’d noted earlier. Since she went behind the first door in the hallway, he didn’t need to move to keep an eye on her. Instead, he slipped his phone into his cargo pocket, then scritched Clio along her lower jaw, thankful for the way the cat soothed his thoughts about his family.

Clio stretched her neck to afford him better access.

Aww. Getting a cat moved to the top of his list, right after purchasing a car.

CHAPTER 9

Tabby shut her laptop and sat back in her thickly padded office chair. The effort to appear unconcerned while trying to remember all the data she'd pulled on the agency, plus confidently answer the partner's question about why she left her last job, pulled just about every ounce of energy left. She covered her face with her hands and took a deep, steadying breath.

How could her life have gone this far off the rails? She'd thought she recovered after Archer's betrayal and constant shenanigans. Draining the joint bank account. Selling their house on Lake LBJ out from under her one week prior to her serving him papers. Cheating on her. Sending false allegations to her job. Those were just the biggies.

She straightened. But now, someone sabotaged her life—they could've left her entire world in literal ashes. Hell. In rural central Texas, a fire had the ability to devastate entire communities. Even if they didn't want to burn down her barn or home, the irresponsibility ignited a hard fury in her, one that balled in her stomach and gave her purpose to find the creep. At least Fernald had acted before anything horrible happened.

Fernald. Even though she'd been screaming at him, he'd saved her home. He'd saved *her* from a serious accident the night before. He'd been gentle when he pulled the thorns from her feet. While they still smarted, she didn't think any trace of them remained. Plus, he didn't comment that she was "being a baby" or that she needed to remove them herself. He even offered to drive her to the med ward.

Tall, dark, and no longer boring. And while Yvette's words of encouragement helped so much to lift her spirits, Fernald's simple comments and can-do attitude inspired her confidence to soar.

Though she'd aimed high for a position at this agency, the most prestigious in Texas, Tabby believed she had a shot, based on the body language and comments from the partner. Her luck had to turn sometime, and it might as well be now.

Deep voices filtered in from outside her office and the tiny bit of joy faded like a snuffed-out candle. Had something happened? Perhaps the lack of crashing and thumps meant Fernald had the matter corralled.

She rose from her comfy perch. Phew. Without another MendMe, she'd taken some over-the-counter pain relievers, and the fiery stabs had receded to irritation. She crossed to the door and peeked out, careful to not make a sound in case she'd been wrong about the voices.

Mouse leaned his butt against the peninsula, one ankle crossed over the other. He shared his height with his half-brother, along with the cheekbones and wavy black hair, which he kept far shorter and wore with a trimmed beard. Though he had a rock-solid build, instead of shifting into a gargoyle like his father, he took after his mother, a wolf shifter, though he seemed more mountain-man bearish to Tabby.

Fernald sat in her grandfather's old recliner, bent forward with his forearms on his thighs. Perhaps feeling the weight of her stare, he looked up, and his teal blue irises glowed bright, intense, as if seeing her for the first time as a desirable woman.

Heat rose to her cheeks, and she couldn't have uttered a word like she was captive to a spell he had spun. Her body tightened and her pulse began to thrum.

He rose to his full, glorious height and held out a hand. "You need a ride over?"

While his words broke her stupor, for a moment she didn't comprehend his meaning—her feet. She mentally shook off the sensual haze that had engulfed her. With a small laugh she continued into the room and sank into the second easy chair, determined to get her wild reaction to him under control. "No. I'm fine. They're just tender now."

Mouse quirked a brow at his brother, but Fernald asked, "How'd it go?"

"Good, I think." She lifted her shoulders in a "who knows?" fashion but then straightened them. At her last agency, she'd had the largest client roster with the biggest book of business. "They said they'll do a second round of interviews, and I'm hoping for a callback."

"You'll get one." His wide smile added to the confidence in his tone. "I know your luck is about to change."

His comment echoed her earlier thought. She'd never gotten support like this from her ex. Even at the outset, he'd always somehow framed her success in terms of him—*his* talented girlfriend, the people *he* introduced her to. Then in the marriage, his money, his house, his vehicles, when in reality, he'd used *her* credit with First Bank of Enchanted Rock, *her* money in the bank account, and what *her* grandma left her in the safety deposit box to fund his lavish lifestyle.

Ugh. Enough of Archer. In fact, all of those nasty memories needed to be put in the burn barrel with the rest of the weeds. Her gaze slid to the gargoyle next to her. Funny how if she got this job, Fernald would've been part of the reason why, though she doubted he even realized his importance.

Mouse cleared his throat, and she startled. Holy hell. She'd forgotten the shifter stood across from her. "Sorry—what brings you here?"

He cut his gaze to his brother, then back to her with a snarky grin. "Since Prada thinks you should come to the Rock just to be a little bit safer, I'm loaning Hudson here a ride."

Hudson? He'd nodded toward his brother. Fernald? Might be a middle name, but Fernald Hudson Grayson didn't quite roll off the tongue. Perhaps a Hebert Security nickname? The first time she'd seen him at Thelma's months ago, he seemed to be on the edge of the group. Over the handful of times since then, his interactions seemed easier, though this was the first time she'd heard a nickname like all but the owner had. Good for Fernald. Rock Hudson or the river or even the movie *Hudson Hawk*, didn't matter.

She skipped the nickname question for later and raised her eyebrows toward Mouse signaling she didn't believe he came here merely to loan a car. For his response, she employed more than her empathic abilities. She'd minored in psychology and employed observation of body language as well. *Fat lot of good it did with Ar—nope, not going to even think of him any longer.*

"Okay, I'm doing double duty." He spread his hands at waist-level. "Copilot to make sure everything goes smoothly."

Her blood turned cold. Truth sang in his body language, then in the emotion behind his words, however much he shaded them to calm her. Danger still lurked. For a little while, she'd pretended to be a confident, modern woman who could handle her problems. Reality said differently. But for Fernald, her home might have been destroyed, and she might have lost her life. The being could still be stalking her and turn to violence if he couldn't find whatever he sought. Goosebumps broke out across her body, and her gaze darted to the windows, the sliding glass door where a cloaked person could be lurking. No tell-tale shadow gave away a hidden figure. *Nothing there, scaredy-cat.*

Clio had sidled up to Fernald for more pets, and he obliged with gentle glides from her head to her shoulder. "I always anticipate trouble. Do I think they're watching? Yes. Do I believe we'll be attacked? Odds are lower if we have him with us."

His steady, sure tone and open body language assuaged much of her fear. "Okay, I'll change. Shouldn't be more than fifteen minutes."

"You might want to pack a bag. We could be gone for a couple of days before this is cleared up." The apologetic tone Fernald employed suggested he wished he didn't have to tell her.

Whoever did this chased her from her home, from her refuge. Her frustration simmered, and she managed a jerky nod in acknowledgement before she spun. While she wanted to march back to her room, her feet wouldn't allow the show of pique, and she'd already screamed to the heavens like a wild woman earlier. She sucked the emotion back and went to pack.

Mental outfit-math worked out to two formal outfits for interviews and a potential in-person call-back, casual clothing, sleepwear, toiletries. Ugh. While she gathered the belongings she'd need, she went over the ways she could make whoever did this's life a living hell. The often-childish scenarios became ridiculous enough that she had to laugh. None, like being forced to be strapped to the backend of a farty troll, would probably ever come true, but she had to have faith that Fernald would keep her safe, and Yvette would put the one who did this in jail. She returned to the den in a considerably better mood.

Yet ensconced in the back of Mouse's big, black, double-cab truck, a pang made her glance over her shoulder while driving away. The 1970s, single-story, yellow brick ranch sorely needed a new roof, paint on the trim, and freshening inside, but it was *her* home. Would this be the last time she saw the house as is?

Anxiety clutched her heart in a grip so tight she couldn't breathe. A sob threatened, but she kept her lips pressed tight. She should've brought Clio. Mouse and Fernald convinced her the perpetrator didn't seem intent on destroying her home, so she'd opted to put extra kibble in Clio's bowl and unlock the doors, hoping against hope that if they entered her house again, they'd pull the door shut and Clio would be safe.

Dammit. She should've spent money on wards. She'd been prioritizing a new car and some updates to the hopelessly dated house, but the paranormal protection system rose to the top of her list. Today even. Perhaps the company had a payment plan.

Fernald made a call to Yvette to let her know he and Tabby were on their way. After he hung up, he said, "She's sent out a Rook to keep tabs on us."

Since Mouse seemed to understand by the tone of his grunt-style acknowledgement, she didn't ask what exactly Yvette meant, but relief trickled through her at the idea NACS would also be watching. A tense silence formed. Rather than try to fill the void with the babblings forming on the tip of her tongue, she determined that Fernald and his brother concentrating on potential threats would be the better use of their attention.

Worry made her shoulders stiff. Every shadow and vehicle she saw became a potential attacker until she had to close her eyes for a bit before she went crazy with anxiety. For several minutes, she forced herself to perform breathing exercises and tried to trust the professionals to do their job.

Finally, Fernald turned onto the larger Highway 281, and the stress in her shoulders began to ease. Surely they would be much safer on the US route, rather than the smaller, two-lane road. She focused on the brothers in the front seats. Fernald manned the wheel because he used to routinely drive for his lord, which apparently included some wild skills. From what she could observe in the rearview mirror, Fernald scanned both the road, what he could see in his mirrors, and his side of their flank, while Mouse did mostly the same from his position but added overhead.

An oppressive pall hung on her shoulders, almost like someone watched her. She turned to look out the wide back window, where a large, black SUV followed at a distance. Even with the overhead sun, she could discern the headlights had the blue-white glare similar to the SUV that nearly mowed over her car the night prior. A cold shiver slithered down her back.

"Hey, um, that black SUV…?"

Mouse dipped his head, possibly checking out the side mirror while Fernald connected his gaze with hers via the rearview. "He's been with us for a while, right after we turned onto the Farm to Market. Dumbass. A sedan would've been more discreet."

Wow. These guys were good. That was a solid ten minutes, and she hadn't noticed. Though not a security professional, she'd been trying to be aware of her surroundings.

The corners of Fernald's eyes crinkled. "Good catch though. He's been doing a pretty good job of using cars to shield himself."

His warm regard melted her feelings of inadequacy, and

she ducked her head in case he saw her ridiculously happy smile. "Thanks."

"We've already texted his plates to your friend," Mouse said almost absently. "Whoever is monitoring overhead for NACS should have his position."

Fernald said "rook" earlier. A raven shifter? At least someone was watching out for them.

The interior returned to silence until Fernald guided the truck off the US highway and onto a smaller state route once more. She tried to peptalk herself that the smaller road meant closer to safety. Just a short sprint to the turnoff only paranormals with access to the Rock could see and they'd be under the granite dome in about ten minutes.

Thank goodness. She was going to have to save for a massage because her stress level—

An explosion rocked the back of the truck and slammed her against the door.

CHAPTER 10

Despite the fishtail skids, Fernald somehow kept the vehicle on the road and racing toward safety. Another violent explosion shattered the window next to Tabitha, and she screamed again.

He had to keep going to protect her. "Mouse."

His brother didn't need further instruction. "Come on up front and get buckled in. This might get hairier soon." Mercifully, the older model truck had an armrest that acted either like a console or a could be lifted to form a seat's back. She jammed herself between him and Mouse, then applied the lap belt. The warmth of her shoulder and hip pressing against his comforted him. She'd survive whatever happened.

No sooner had she clicked the buckle than another explosion slammed against his eardrums and tossed the truck into the air. Fighting the bucking movements, he struggled to get his arm around her shoulders, finally able to pin her next to him while the pickup rolled over and over. Her purse smashed into his head, and the spilled contents circled the cabin.

He lost count of the rolls before the truck landed on its top.

No time to waste. He had to get her moving because whoever pursued them would probably come looking. "You two okay?"

"I'mma kill me someone." The hard, mean tone said Mouse meant bad business, and Fernald shared his sentiment.

"I'm okay," Tabitha said, her voice a little woozy. He didn't think she hit her head again, but the tumbles might've disoriented her.

"If you can move, we need to get out, now."

"I think I can." Her voice had become stronger, but if she couldn't he'd carry her.

He unwound himself and upon release of his belt, folded to the floor. He hastily righted himself, then helped Tabitha from her awkward suspension by her hips. A quick glance around determined the truck landed next to uncleared land. The trees and scrubby bushes would help hide them. Hissing from the pickup precluded any listening for others, and the black smoke and gasoline odors overpowered his sense of smell.

"Come on sweetling, away from the truck. Keep low."

He pulled his phone from his thigh pocket and with his other hand grabbed Tabitha's wrist. At least she'd dressed in tennis shoes and jeans. Though the thick brush probably concealed cactus and mesquite, the spines would still be safer than waiting for whoever chased them to show up.

Movement at his side almost made him draw the gun he'd secured in his waistband holster but proved to be his brother. Good thing. He unlocked his phone and dialed Prada.

"Where are you?" Her voice was clipped and urgent.

Just left Highway 281 and they hit us with something that rolled the car. We're on foot, headed," he hazarded a glance up, "west."

"Okay, Rook has you in his sights. We're almost there."

"Stop or I'll shoot." The male voice sounded from behind.

Fuck that. He would protect Tabitha. She slowed, then stumbled along with a snarled curse when Fernald kept going. Mouse would handle the threat.

He shoved his phone into his thigh pocket. When he entered a small clearing, he shifted, wings bursting from his back, and scooped her into his arms without any explanation. He needed to get her out of here now.

A deep, authoritative voice came from his right and said, "Halt or I'll kill her."

His training said keep going, but instinct and the flat, deadly tone of the speaker made Fernald glance to his right. Five weapons pointed at him and Tabitha. No one wore NACS gear. All but one wore balaclavas. From the ski masks, hard, teal-blue gazes said gargoyle. Worst of all, the tallest of the group, the one not in a uniform, Fernald recognized from Lord Regus's dealings.

Griffith Jenkins. One of the most violent, successful gangsters in the paranormal world.

The oversized fae had to have troll blood added to his primarily goblin heritage. Bigger than a gargoyle, meaner than a goblin, smarter than an elf. The fae had a ragged scar down one cheek and a perturbingly urbane grin that matched his tailored pinstriped suit. He motioned to the masked males around him, each bearing two large-caliber guns, no doubt primed with rounds spelled to not only penetrate gargoyle hide, but to keep the victim from healing.

But Fernald didn't worry about his own skin. He may heal like most paranormals. Tabitha might not.

With this split-second diagnosis of the situation, Fernald stopped and shoved her behind him.

"I have a simple question for Ms. McBee, and we'll be on our way." Jenkins's conversational tone belied the cold menace in his voice. "Where's the Bracelet of Belief?"

She flinched, but Fernald's wings held her cocooned behind him. The gangster wanted the old fae relic? The magical item hadn't been seen in millennia and had probably been lost to time.

Jenkins's frown gave him that heavy-browed goblin look. "Come now, Ms. McBee. We don't have time to waste. Answer and you can stay with your boyfriend."

Fernald kept his expression even. The bait of leaving unharmed wasn't worth Tabitha's life.

She stepped from behind Fernald, and he wrapped a protective arm around her quaking shoulders. If needed, he'd turn to take a barrage of bullets. He itched to draw the gun Mouse delivered to him earlier, but Jenkins had a strange type of honor and would usually keep his word.

"I-I don't know what you're talking about." Her voice shook, perhaps well understanding the danger.

Nevertheless, Jenkins's grin turned sour. "Sure you do. He said he slipped it into your bag when he ran into you last night. The bracelet's worth a great deal to me, and Mr. Eskew said he couldn't find it when he searched your house."

"Archer?" She practically spit the name onto the ground. She straightened and began to shake. "That's who's doing this? Oh my god. Now I know why he seemed familiar. His voice—he took a New ID potion didn't he?"

Fury rocketed through Fernald. The ex definitely needed an attitude adjustment, and Fernald would give him a good one once he'd gotten her to safety.

The giant fae took a menacing step forward. "Where is the relic?"

"I don't have the bracelet and don't know what happened to the damned thing. What I can tell you is he's a liar through and through." The fury in her tone carried the force of a volcanic eruption.

Fernald was proud of her bravery, since this gangster had made many piss their pants in terror. But waving a red cape in front of this bull could have dire consequences. He squeezed her closer.

"Are you sure Archer didn't sell it out from under you?"

Jenkins's expression turned mean, perhaps at her scornful tone, perhaps with the idea he might've been double-crossed.

Fernald prepared to sweep her behind him, and said, "She's telling the truth. We found no relic." Though he doubted his statement would bear any weight, he had to try. Prada should be close. *Buy time.*

Jenkins's hand flexed, and Fernald tensed, prepared to protect Tabby. To the death if necessary.

Wolves and jaguars burst into the clearing from the brush. Gunfire exploded around him. Tabitha dropped to the ground. Fernald covered her with his body and wings. A white-hot fire stabbed him in the wing and ribs, then another in the ass. He gritted his teeth. Damned spelled rounds. Only through long experience with the pernicious things did he master what many would find a debilitating agony. *Protect her*, chanted in his head.

"Guns down. Hands in the air!" The female's voice brooked no argument.

Fernald chanced a glance. Three of the masked goons were on the ground and two stood with hands raised, one of which glared at him. Not surprising. While uniformed NACS officers approached the gangster's group in overwhelming numbers, there was no sign of Jenkins himself. Dammit. He got away?

A woman strode toward him clad in security's black top and pants. Purpose and determination emanated from her in waves. She had a blond streak running down the middle of her dark hair, and added with her ferocious scowl and solid build, she appeared a formidable opponent despite her compact size.

"Tabby!" The voice matched the one on the phone, and relief sung through his veins. This must be Prada.

Tabitha tried to rise. "Over here, Yvette—oof. Get off of me."

"Not until Jenkins's thugs are completely secure." He said that as much for Tabitha as her friend. Though NACS personnel swarmed the scene, those beings were a danger to her.

Without breaking eye contact with him, Prada called over her shoulder toward the officers. "Secure?"

"Secure, ma'am," one of the officers shouted back.

With reluctance, Fernald rose. He couldn't account for Jenkins. Once standing, he helped Tabitha to her feet, ensuring he stood between her and the mobster's crew. He expected her to race to her friend, but instead, she wrapped her arm around his middle and hugged him to her side.

Though he nearly gasped at the pain since her arm came close to one of his wounds, an ocean of emotions swamped him, from surprise at her staying with him, to gratefulness for her survival, to anger she'd been put in the precarious position, to…caring. Too soon for love surely, but he wanted to know much more about the remarkable woman who stood with him. The bullets didn't hit anything major like a heart or lung. He could wait for attention until Tabitha was away from the scene.

A corner of Prada's lips quirked. "You okay?"

Adding a slow nod, Tabitha glanced up to him and said, "Yeah. Thanks to Fernald."

His breath hitched and his mouth dried at the tenderness in her gaze and her soft smile. Then she blinked and turned her focus back to her friend. "And Mouse too. Where is he? What in the hell has been going on, Yvette?"

Prada's gaze ping-ponged between him and Tabitha. Then the shorter woman crossed her arms while a muscle worked in her jaw. "Mouse is fine. This has been driving me crazy because I didn't get the go to tell you about it until too late. I really hate the blood oath sometimes."

Fernald understood Prada's dilemma, however much his frustration simmered at the fact she didn't disclose what danger faced her friend. He'd been the subject of one of those oaths and betraying the spell took extreme skill. Failure to abide by the spell's rules became agonizing, one hundred times worse than the magical ammunition.

"I can't tell you until after a debrief." Prada shook her head in the negative. "I need both of you not to discuss this with each other or anyone else until after the interview."

"Fine. But then I get everything." Her fingers clamped down, and he tensed against the unintentional pain she caused. She glanced up at him, her brow gathered.

He didn't move fast enough to avoid her discovery of the hole in his shirt and dampness from blood still seeping from the injury since the spell wouldn't allow for healing. Dammit. He'd hoped not to worry her.

"You're hurt." Her voice rose, adding an edge of panic. She scooted around him and said to her friend, "You need to get a medic. And here's another gunshot. Yvette, hurry."

Fortunately, her fingers flitted over the fabric at his butt. He turned to Tabitha, whose eyes were wide, and she'd snagged her lower lip between her teeth. Tenderly, he raised his hand to cup her cheek. "I'm okay."

Tears lined her lower lashes. "But you're still bleeding and aren't healing. Don't gargoyles heal like shifters?"

"Yes, but not against the spelled rounds. My gargoyle skin

slows the penetration down tremendously. The medics should have a counter-spell. I'll be fine." He framed her shoulders with his hands and tried to soothe her agitation with light thumb strokes.

"Gun," a woman shouted from over Tabitha's shoulder.

One of the gargoyles had somehow freed themselves and shook off a security officer.

No! He'd allowed her to be exposed. He shoved her aside and dove to cover her once more. But the now unmasked and smiling gargoyle—his father—had already fired.

Searing agony lit his head, then blackness.

CHAPTER 11

Fernald's full weight fell onto Tabby and robbed her of air. More gunshots rang out. Yells and snarling too. While she tried to recover her breath, the commotion ended. He pinned her into the hard, sunbaked ground, immobilizing her arms and legs. Her cheek rested on a rough rock. "Hey. You're squishing me."

"Don't move, Tabby. Medic! Now!" Yvette yelled with a high edge to her voice.

Tabby froze. Her friend wouldn't panic for no reason. "What's happening? Fernald?"

No response.

She moved her elbow enough to lightly poke his ribs. "Fernald?"

When she received no response, she pushed again and said his name. Razor-sharp fear shredded her heart. She shoved and called for him. Why wasn't he responding?

Gradually she became cognizant that a hand gripped the edge of her elbow, and Yvette said, "Hey, girl. He'll be alright. Shh."

A small part of Tabby understood she wasn't helping the

situation by panicking. *Breathe.* After two deep, hiccupping breaths, his weight lifted from her.

She scrambled to right herself.

"Nope." Yvette swiftly grabbed Tabby's shoulders and turned her until she had her back to Fernald.

She had to make sure he lived. Trying to see over her shoulder, she twisted, but her friend's grip held firm.

"Don't." Yvette's features smoothed in a calm mask. "You don't want to see this right now. He'll be fine. I promise."

If only those last two sentences sounded like she believed them, Tabby might relax. If she shouldn't see him, the injury had to be bad. She pictured the blood, then thrust aside the image and forced herself to swallow the horror. With her throat so raw, her voice sounded agonized and alien to her own ears when she whispered, "What happened?"

Yvette's lips firmed, and she exhaled a short, swift breath. "He was shot in the head."

Time seemed to slow. Instead of revulsion and nausea, fury licked through her veins. Motion over Yvette's shoulder caught Tabby's attention.

A security officer led hand-cuffed Archer toward a mage's portal. He tipped his head back and laughed—laughed!—at something one of the NACS personnel said. White rage edged her vision. If he hadn't put the stupid relic in her purse, she wouldn't be here, and Fernald would be fine.

Time swerved and resumed its regular pace. She wrenched herself from her friend's arms, raced toward her ex-husband, and screamed his name.

Archer looked over his shoulder and his eyes widened.

Someone grabbed her from behind, then another stepped in front of her. She fought to free herself, her only desire an animalistic need to hurt the man who had been the catalyst for hurting Fernald, but the hands that held her remained fast.

An officer pushed Archer through the portal, and the large sparkling circle slammed shut with a loud pop.

All fight seemed to evaporate. Tabby sagged, panting. The officer stepped aside, and arms wrapped around her shoulders. Yvette held her, but Tabby was too exhausted and heartsick to even cry. For who knows how long she wallowed in her misery and anger and fear.

"We've stabilized him, and we're getting ready to move him," a male voice from behind her said.

The words galvanized Tabby, and she straightened. "I'll go with him,"

"You can't," Yvette said, her voice unexpectedly gentle.

Her emotion's bartender added frustration to her current cocktail. Tabby crossed her arms. "What do you mean, I can't?"

"We need to get your statement."

The patience in Yvette's tone only added to Tabby's aggravation. "For fuck's sake, now?"

"I wish it didn't have to be now." Yvette canted her head a little. "I can tell this guy means a lot to you. Besides, you can't stay while they're working on him. We'll do everything we can. Regardless of if that happens or not—"

"Are you saying he might die?" Yvette's oblique reference iced Tabby's blood.

Her voice came out louder than she intended. Over her friend's shoulder, several officers swiveled their gaze toward the conversation, but Tabby didn't care.

Yvette held up her hands at chest level and said with a stern evenness Tabby had never heard before, "Nothing is ever certain. Regardless, we need your statement to help convict that sorry sack of carbon and water you call an ex-husband. I think your Grayson would want that. I'm not saying we do or don't have enough evidence to do so. But your statement is important."

The conflict threw cold water on Tabby's burning anger—put the hurt on Archer or be with Fernald. "You'd tell me if I needed to be with him, right?"

"Absolutely."

Yvette's simple word and direct eye contact cemented Tabby's decision. They had been friends for almost twenty years. The wolverine shifter was her fiercest friend and someone who wouldn't steer her wrong.

She glanced over her friend's shoulder to where a magical medic motioned with his hands and the stretcher holding Fernald levitated several feet off the ground. His head had been wrapped in white bandages and her heart trembled with the knowledge that but for her, he never would have been in the situation.

Though she hated the logic, if he'd been shot in the head with a spelled bullet, Fernald wouldn't be aware of his surroundings for at least the next couple of hours. She straightened her shoulders and set aside her worry for now.

She had to believe she would have time to apologize to him and for more than calling him boring.

~

Tabby sat in a sterile, boxy room at a table whose chipped, scratched finish spoke of long years and sad stories. No one came here for a good time, only because something bad had happened, usually by them, to them, or to someone they loved. She shifted on the chair whose padding had long lost its ability to provide comfort. Much longer and her butt would be asleep.

She'd been in this NACS interview room for what seemed

an eternity but had probably only been about ten minutes. A quick round of breaths had calmed her mind, though she still turned her full coffee cup in careful circles. The constant movement kept her sane. Gargoyles may be the hardiest of the paranormals, capable of regenerating after severe head wounds, but she couldn't banish the worry from her mind and heart.

A tall, raven-haired man entered the room. Another male came behind him, perhaps an inch or two shorter, with wavy chestnut locks.

The first one shot her a sympathetic smile and said, "I'm Dean Rook. I'm an investigator for Clan Shifter Security, but I'm on loan to NACS right now." He hooked a thumb to his right. "This is Warrick Sicaridum."

Dean Rook? The rook in the sky, perhaps? She introduced herself, then the investigators sat in the chairs opposite her. The other officer, who might've been implied to be with shifter security, had the elegant build of another clan—fae, probably. He opened a leather folio he brought with him and clicked a pen's end in apparent readiness to take notes.

"I'm really sorry we have to do this now," Investigator Rook said. "I got an update from the med ward, and they said Grayson will be fine. He'll be out for a day or two. If they do have anything emergent, they promised to notify me immediately."

Could she believe him? Maybe, but security officers meant the males had robust mental barriers. She had to go on his body language and dialogue cues. He set his phone atop the table as if he meant what he'd said. Despite her natural caution, she got a good vibe from the guy, and she relaxed a bit for the first time in the last couple of hours.

"Thank you for the update." She fought against emotion threatening to clog her throat. "He's a good man—gargoyle. He didn't deserve to get shot like that. Not for me."

"No one does. That's why we're here." The shifter's focus sharpened, and while he seemed like a nice person, she had no doubt he would go for the literal jugular if necessary. "Tell me about your day yesterday."

"From the start?" Why not from when her ex ran into her? Despite the waste of time about her rushed morning, after his confirmation about when to start, she humored him. He asked questions about her regular customers, those she didn't know, if she went for lunch, what she did while there were no customers in the boutique.

"You closed the store a bit later than usual?"

Huh. Now she knew why he wanted her to start at the beginning of her day. His questions calmed her and made her memory clearer. He was good at this.

"Yep. I'm guessing around six-thirty. I let out a customer who stayed a bit after the official closing time. When I went to relock the doors, I thought I saw something under the bank eaves across the way. Don't know why they don't put better lighting because the shadows are as dark as a banshee's dress right there."

Investigator Rook quirked a corner of his mouth. "I think new lighting is on the schedule for tomorrow."

"Good. Anyway, I thought Fer—"

Oh shit. He *was* good. Got her so comfortable she mentioned what she hadn't told Yvette. Her cheeks heated and there wasn't a damn thing she could do to stop her reaction. A tell-tale fractional lift of his brows told her he'd caught her slip. Now, she'd have to tell the truth. She explained how Mouse had asked Fernald to watch over the shop. "I thought the shadow might've been him. I didn't mention it to Yvette because, well, I didn't want her to think he might be responsible."

Ugh. The explanation sounded worse than she thought.

"Why didn't you want her to think he was involved?" This came from the other investigator, who studied her through narrowed eyes.

Damn him for the question. She couldn't squirm out with a lie. Just the facts. "I'm attracted to him, and I didn't want him to be involved, and I didn't want a bunch of questions like these that made me feel like a girl drawing hearts around initials in her notebook during third period history class."

The sarcasm she added to her long-winded answer earned her a smothered snicker from Investigator Rook, but the other male didn't crack a smile. "You don't think he's involved?"

"Come on. Me versus him? He could've just taken the bracelet from me with zero effort and eliminated me as a witness."

"Okay." Investigator Sicaridum scribbled something in his notebook. Hopefully, whatever he wrote didn't damage Fernald.

"What happened next?" the shifter prompted.

At the end of her story, she had to drink some of the nasty cold coffee—with her dry mouth, she couldn't imagine talking for at least another two days. Investigator Rook had glanced at his phone a couple of times but said nothing about Fernald. Tabby kept her metaphorical fingers and toes crossed that he pulled through. Her soul hurt that she was the cause of this.

Investigator Rook shook his head. "Looks like you were lucky. Not many people draw the attention of Griffith Jenkins and walk away unscathed."

"I think Fernald would beg to differ," she said with a sharp tone dryer than West Texas dirt in summer. "What was this Bracelet of Belief supposed to do, anyway?"

"It's supposed to bring the possessor good luck, but in reality, the magic tricks them into thinking they are invincible, which inevitably, they discover is untrue." The shifter shook his head, his features wry.

"That's plain weird. How did Archer get involved?"

"We'd heard Jenkins was looking for the relic. We happened to have access. Since he's wanted for breaking out of prison, we thought we had a good opportunity to draw him out and capture him. Your ex owed him a lot of money, and Jenkins thought he could leverage Eskew's ability for burglaries. He's moved up in the trade if he can knock off a bank."

For a moment, her thoughts couldn't form coherently, then she said, "I found out he'd conned people out of money. A *lot* of money. That was the last straw for me. I didn't know he had taken to burglaries. But it makes sense he'd use his telekinetic abilities like that."

Now she understood why she'd found her door unlocked last night. He'd probably manipulated the locks. *Oh shit.* Clio. She'd never liked Archer and hissed at him any time he walked into a room. Tabby wanted to bang her head against a wall, but if she'd done that each time she thought of her stupidity in marrying the bastard, she'd probably have a flat spot on her forehead. Initially, her intellect made the decisions in the relationship. She hadn't listened to her instinct until she'd been stuck like a moth in an orb weaver's web.

"Telekinetic? Isn't that interesting?" The shifter slid a glance to his partner, and a silent conversation seemed to be ongoing for a moment.

What did that mean? If only she could read minds beyond her simple empathic skills.

Finally, the other male shook his head, and Investigator Rook returned his focus to the interview. "I don't think that's on his clan registration. Now we know why he's good at getting in and out of places."

Yikes. Failure to disclose abilities could lead to big jail time.

Aww. Poor Archer, a little voice said in a snarky tone. Tabby might've laughed, except a question came to her. "But if he did put the bracelet in my purse, where did it go? *I* don't have the damn thing."

The shifter's grin turned predatory, and he waggled his phone before putting the device back on the table. "Just got an update on that. Turns out he decided to see what Jenkins wanted so badly. He opened the lead-lined box, and the bracelet came to m—"

"Ahem." Investigator Sicaridum shot a pointed glare to his partner.

Definitely a conversation.

Rook said, "And it went to a lodestone last night around midnight."

Now where had she heard that term before? Oh yeah. She'd taken History of the Fae at Enchanted Rock University as an elective. Certain beings, regardless of clan, operated like an old-fashioned magnet for some magical fae artifacts. If not handled properly, like stored in a lead-lined box, the item might travel on its own.

She shot the shifter a look but didn't voice her suspicion *he* was the referenced lodestone. Nor did she voice her satisfaction that her ex's own greed sunk him.

"When we arrested him, he had the box and admitted he'd broken into your house to recover it from your purse, but got frantic when he couldn't find the bracelet."

No wonder her tote had been so heavy last night. "I hope you plan on adding assault of both me and Fernald, as well as burglary of my home to Archer's charges."

"With pleasure." Investigator Rook's grin turned feral.

Air suddenly seemed not enough, and she got lightheaded. After years of feeling like she could barely keep her head above water, her feet had found the bottom. Archer

Eskew would be publicly known for the shitty person he was, not the smooth playboy he portrayed to the world. Karma didn't need Tabby's help after all. The feeling that she'd finally shaken a lingering cancer swept through her, but she had one more thing hanging over her head.

"What about Jenkins? I don't think you arrested him. He could still think I know where the relic is."

Investigator Rook formed his hand into a fist for a fleeting second before he relaxed his grip. "He escaped, unfortunately. We'll circulate the information that we're in possession and that you never really had the bracelet. He'll believe us, otherwise, you'd use or sell it, since the relic is quite valuable in certain circles."

Now she stood on dry land, free of this business. "Good. Any more questions?"

After glancing at the other man who swiveled his head from side to side, the shifter said, "Nothing else, but we may have some follow-up later."

When she rose, she felt a curious lightness, one similar to the optimism after her job interview.

Perhaps her luck *was* changing.

Perhaps she needed to listen to the little voice that told her she should take a chance on a gargoyle who made her feel good, one who enjoyed gardening like she did, one who definitely didn't bear the "boring" brand.

Perhaps she needed to ask Fernald to dinner.

CHAPTER 12

Fernald stared at the pink granite overhead and tried to conserve energy. Everything seemed in place. He could feel the cool cotton coverlet over his toes and under his fingers. By the machines attached to the walls and the other bed in the room, he lay in the med ward.

Where was Tabitha?

His father tried to kill her. Rage exploded within Fernald and only with supreme effort did he restrain himself from trying to throw off the sheet, find that asshole, and finally end him the only way he could—cutting off his head since Fernald didn't have access to lightning.

Instead, he slowed his breathing and pushed aside his worry about the woman he wanted more than any other. *Heal.* Was that Linden's voice?

He slipped back into darkness.

When he woke again, he kept his eyes closed and breathed deeply. Good. Still on Earth and not flying with the gods.

His acute hearing picked up breathing and he opened his lids, hoping for the beautiful woman for whom he'd risk everything.

Instead of Tabitha, a male sat in the chair next to the bed, and another rested his shoulder against the wall across from Fernald. He didn't recognize either and tensed in preparation for defense. The one standing held up his hand and flashed a badge. "I'm Dean Rook with Shifter Security on loan to NACS. This is Warrick Sicaridum."

Interesting the shifter hadn't given the same provenance to his partner. *Sicaridum.* Fernald recognized the name. Sprite. Was he on NACS business, too, or did he have his own agenda?

Fernald lifted his head in acknowledgement to both, but sent a sharp look to Sicaridum, one he hoped said he recognized the sprite—the queen's foremost assassin. Always puzzles within games within riddles with the fae. Fernald had no desire to play them anymore. He'd been a pawn in them for far too long.

Any fight left him and he settled back to his bed. Not like he could probably defeat either of the two right now. Best to conserve his energy. Besides, he had a question. "Where's Tabitha?"

Sicaridum lifted a brow. "Doc said she left a while ago to get wards installed at her house."

Relief surged through him. Hopefully she got the best. If not, he'd help her pay for whatever she needed for the premium protection.

When Fernald didn't respond, Rook said, "We're here about the events that happened four days ago regarding Ms. McBee."

Four days ago? How long had he been out? "Where do you want me to start?"

"Start with Wednesday. How'd you start your day?"

Though others in his past preferred torture to gain the truth, Fernald understood the investigator's purpose behind the question. He provided what the two wanted without prevarication or shading. The faster they had their answers, the faster he could finish healing and go find Tabitha.

"Your own father shot you?" Sicaridum didn't look up but continued writing in his notebook.

"Yes. I had heard he was working for the Sunda's, but I guess rumor got the info half right—criminal organization, but the wrong one. I'm just glad he'll be in prison. If you got three more Graysons, they're probably my brothers." They'd made their bed and could burn in it.

The corner of the shifter's mouth quirked. "Got two of them, then. Rumor also says that Jenkins is pissed that your pops shot at her without approval and put out a contract on him. If so, he won't last long."

Every stronghold held weaknesses. Most of Chinati Maximum Security Prison's vulnerabilities were on two feet. Somehow, Jenkins's bounty would be spread. Fernald tried to dredge up some pity, but his father had beaten that out of him years ago. "Is that all?"

"For now." Rook straightened. "You going to continue with Hebert Security?"

"Maybe." That was the first untruth he'd given. Violence had never appealed to him. After his release, he worked for Nathan Hebert's security company more as a way make money and stall for time until he decided what he wanted to do. "If you can't find me, my half-brother will know how to reach me."

Once the two had left the room, he settled back, his eyelids heavy. Sleep. He needed to heal. He closed his lids and drifted, his body heavy with exhaustion.

Trees. None were quite like those in Lanorinia, though those on Earth had their own beauty. He stood in a grove of silkwood with its gray papery bark and tall, arching branches soaring overhead thick with velvety leaves. A stream burbled nearby, one from the far edges of Lord Regus's estate. He'd visited this place both in his childhood and in his dreams.

He breathed deeply of the air he thought he'd never inhale again, the overhead sun warming the breeze, the crisp delicate fragrance of crushed sugar grass under his feet, its lush green dotted with rare, sweet, starlight blossoms. Every time he saw the flowers, his heart constricted for the poor kitten and the way her life ended. If only he hadn't shown his younger brother. Never again had he given anyone knowledge that could be used against him.

Wake up. He hated this dream and the memories he'd find. *Wake up now.*

The faintest rumbling met his ears just before pressure slid along his leg. He glanced down and he couldn't breathe.

Starlight. She'd never appeared in his dreams before. Slowly, he reached down to scoop her up, afraid this was merely a trick, and she'd turn into a hissing rock serpent or some other evil beast. When he brought her to his eye level, the tiny animal with her soft, fuzzy fur and bright blue eyes bumped her forehead against his chin. Why had she appeared to him now?

"She waited for you. We both have."

Though he recognized the voice, he shielded the kitten against trickery when he pivoted.

Linden, Lord Regus's gardener, sat on one of the flat rocks along the glen's edge, his large, gnarled hands stacked atop a carved walking stick. He appeared much the same as when Fernald last saw him nearly eighty years ago. He wore a pair of work-worn brown trousers, a lighter brown shirt, and a leaf-green jacket. His leather boots were scuffed in the most comfortable way, not unlike his features—kind, careworn, and browned by the sun.

"Looks like you're ready, Fernald." The old brownie's voice had always been a musical baritone and had only deepened with time.

"Ready for what?"

"For your new life. One of your choosing. No more fighting, no more destruction." Linden stood slowly using his stick, then he hobbled over to stand before Fernald, who wanted to ask a hundred questions, but none would emerge.

The old brownie carefully took the kitten into his arms without a protest, cradling the wee thing, which had begun to purr even louder. His eyes twinkled, and his iridescent double wings rose, fluttered, then beat with a rough hum. "You know what you want to do."

"What if it doesn't work out?" The words burst from Fernald's lips in more of a croak.

Linden placed his hand on Fernald's shoulder. "Then cut yourself loose and begin again, my boy."

"Wait. This isn't a dream?"

"Never has been." Linden lifted from the ground, hovering, Starlight peeking over his arm.

The peaceful glen had always seemed too perfect, too real. Holy hell. He projected his conscious mind. Though elves and fairies had been known to possess the gift, Fernald hadn't known gargoyles could. He took in the brownie and ensured he committed every detail to memory. "I won't see you again."

"No. Not until it's your time to fly with the gods. Live well, Fernald. You deserve your time."

Fernald tracked the brownie until the sun's bright orb obscured his friend.

For a moment, Fernald stood with a heart inexplicably both full and empty of joy. He crossed to the rock where Linden had rested and closed his eyes, focusing on the leaves rustling in the gentle breeze and the water laughingly making its way downstream. The air ripe with rich, verdant grass, and perfumed by the starlight flowers. Would he ever see this again?

Finally, the question he knew he couldn't avoid any longer pushed to the front of his mind. What did *he* want to do? No more fighting, no more destruction.

Creation. He wanted to make something fresh. Build a new life.

With Tabitha?

He rubbed the back of his neck. At least he'd like to explore the possibility. Her intriguing mix of determination and free-spirited vivaciousness called to him. Tempted him to emerge from the stony cocoon he'd build around himself to keep him from feeling, from expressing anything that would be destroyed by his life's cruelty.

Tempted him to be who he was meant to be.

He opened his eyes and emerged from the not-dream. He inhaled deeply, refreshed unlike he'd experienced in his ninety-odd years. A whisper of movement came from his left, and he turned his head.

Tabitha sat in the chair next to the bed. She wore a red suit jacket, and she'd pulled her hair back in a sleek, twisted fashion.

He'd never seen anything more beautiful in his life. "You look nice."

"You look horrible." An impish grin crossed her lips, and she fairly vibrated with energy. "And I'm glad you're going to be okay. I had an interview today."

"With the place from the first interview or one of the next day's—what is that, yesterday?"

"The Jenkins thing was four days ago." Her rouged lips grinned wide. "The agency from the first interview called me back. I think the in-person went even better and that I have a shot. Thanks to you."

"I didn't do anything."

"You may not think so. But your encouragement really helped."

He tried to recall what he'd said, but he could only remember a joke about her slippers and telling her she'd do great. "Trust me, it was all you."

"Not going to argue." She shook her head from side to side with a playful grin, which faded quickly. "Enough about me. How do you feel?"

"Better. In fact, I think the best I've felt in a long time." He didn't know what he'd done to deserve this chance, but he'd grab the handle and hold on for dear life.

She nibbled on her lip and clutched her hands in her lap tightly enough that they'd gone white.

"Is there something wrong?"

"I want to apologize for, well, everything."

"Why? None of what happed was your fault."

"No, except for Archer putting the relic in my purse thinking he might be followed, he wouldn't have attacked you, and you wouldn't have been shot." She winced. "I can't imagine being shot in the head."

"Happened a couple of times." The comment slipped out before he edited his thoughts.

She rocked forward with a gasp and put her warm, soft hand on his shoulder, eyes wide. "Good grief. How horrible."

"Not fun." Now was not the time to go into what had been. Now was the time for new beginnings. He took the plunge.

"If you really want to make it up to me, would you consider a dinner date at the Werehouse?"

Tabitha froze, then swallowed hard.

Shit. She wasn't interested. "Hey, I think I might've misjudged something, and if you don't—"

"Yes. I would like to go to dinner with you." Her voice echoed in the med ward's hushed atmosphere, and she winced with a half-smile. "But only if I can apologize."

"None of this is your fault." He pointed to his head.

"Not that. Well, that too, but I called you boring." She slumped against the back of the chair.

The confession stalled any further arguments. "I don't understand."

Her cheeks tinged a pretty rose, and she looked down at her hands. "Thelma pointed you out at Xavier and Brie's barbecue, the one a couple months ago. I had just gotten the final bill from my divorce lawyer and was smarting a little bit." Her gaze lifted and connected with his in a tangle he couldn't unravel. "I told Thelma that you might be handsome, but you were boring. I wanted to apologize. You are probably the least boring person I know."

She thought him handsome, maybe even interesting? He recalled the event, then he laughed. "I'd just accepted the job with Hebert and felt like an awkward outsider to the close-knit group. Probably didn't say a handful of words all night. Add a mumbled introduction to the most attractive woman I'd ever seen and no wonder you thought I was boring."

"Ugh. I feel so juvenile for even telling you, but I'm tired of lies and subterfuge. I want to be open with someone I'm dating—" She sighed and brought her hand to her face.

He might've teased her, but she was already embarrassed enough. Plus, her implication she wanted to date him buoyed his spirits. "Apology accepted."

She took his hand in hers and laced her fingers with his. "Then you better hurry up and get out of here, because we have dinner to go to."

CHAPTER 13

T*wo days later*

Tabby twisted and turned, trying to get a good look at every angle in the crappy big-box store mirror strapped to the back of her bedroom door.

When the painterly-patterned, turquoise chiffon dress arrived at Boutique Magique earlier in the spring with the other samples, she immediately tried it on. The long, wrapped style self-belted at the waist, had long, full sleeves, and a very deep V-neck. While the lines suited her body, the way the fabric moved when she walked made her buy the dress—the cutaway skirt flowed back, revealing a generous amount of her leg with each stride. She loved how the slinky, sexy dress' color made her glow.

What she hadn't loved was the price. Bills needed paying. Besides, where would she wear such a confection? No one had been banging down her door for a date. She put the piece on the rack with the rest of the new garments.

The striking dress sold out quickly, which had been for the best because Tabby had come terribly close to a week-long ramen noodle diet to afford the garment. Yet, a couple of months later, she'd arrived at work after a day off and Thelma told her someone returned the dress, then mentioned she'd be putting it on sale anyway since the summer clothes were already on the floor.

Thelma had held the piece back to save Tabby's pride, of that she possessed no doubt, though she couldn't get her boss to come off the story. With the sale price and the generous employee discount, plus a little cash Tabby had left over at the end of the month, she'd splurged. The gorgeous garment had hung in her closet for almost half a year.

Until tonight.

A pair of barely-there sparkling heels made her legs look gazelle-long and a couple of gold chains layered at her neckline added a delicate emphasis. A low ponytail put the accent on her eyes. Simple makeup completed the outfit. She checked the time using the old-fashioned 1980s digital clock on her nightstand.

Eep—he should be here at any moment. She grabbed her clutch and hurriedly switched the essentials from her regular bag.

A jingling chime announced Fernald crossed her new ward's protection barriers. When she exited her bedroom, she no longer averted her eyes from her grandmother's door. Now it stood open. Though she'd only been able to get through about a quarter of the relatively small main bedroom, Tabby had made a good start. She'd even found a cache of collectible coins dating back to the mid-eighteen hundreds stored in an old vinyl suitcase stuffed under a dresser. If the faded amounts written on the protective covers were anything to judge by, she could have a tidy amount in case of an emergency.

A little thrill shot through her because she wouldn't need the money for day-to-day expenses any longer. She couldn't wait to tell Fernald.

Once she reached the living room, she stopped and took a

couple of centering breaths to counteract the expectation fizzing in her belly. The doorbell rang. She'd expected him to come to the carport, so she pivoted.

When she reached the vestibule, the three small windows set like stair steps in the panel's top half revealed the identity of her visitor, should she have had any question.

After swinging the door wide, she froze. She'd thought Fernald handsome in his casual attire, usually cargo pants and a polo shirt. In his charcoal suit and tie, offset with a crisp, white shirt, he was classically devastating. The cut of his coat emphasized both the breadth of his shoulders and the leanness of his hips, and the pants made her want to do something sinfully decadent and sweaty with him. With a courage she didn't know she possessed, she boldly met his gaze.

Heated masculine appreciation in his eyes made her cheeks flare with warmth and her body go all tingly.

The silence had stretched for several moments when he held out a bouquet of beautiful, white, star-shaped flowers. "These are for you."

The petals had an iridescent sheen, almost as if they twinkled. Their fragrance enticed her, rich, but not cloying. After she accepted them, she brought them to her nose. She'd smelled them once before at a wedding long ago and had never been able to forget their incredible perfume.

Starlight blossoms. Over the top of the small bouquet, her gaze connected to his. They wouldn't grow on Earth, and not many of the cut flowers left the realm due to demand. They didn't flower when cultivated and only grew in certain places within Lanorinia. "They're gorgeous." Her voice had taken on a throaty husk. "Thank you, please come in."

She crossed the house, rooted around in a kitchen cupboard, and managed to find a clear glass vase with the right proportions for the small bouquet.

For now, she set the beautiful flowers on the peninsula. They'd go next to her bed when she got back, where she could stare at their luminescence and fall asleep to the wonderful fragrance.

While she worked, he'd said nothing, seeming happy to watch her. She quirked a brow at him, a mute inquiry at his own silence. He came around the counter and stopped directly in front of her.

She craned her neck to meet his gaze and the intensity in his features took her breath away.

"I used to think that starlights were the most beautiful thing. But I was wrong."

The fizziness in her stomach spread to her blood. Many had told her she was pretty. None had made her feel as rare and treasured as a starlight blossom.

Her gaze dropped to his sensual lips.

"May I?"

"Yes, please." Her voice came out in a breathy, pleading whisper. The intensity in his teal gaze blazed, and she couldn't look away while his head descended toward hers. Finally, her lips met his in a brush, then a claiming, and she shut her lids against the liquid want beginning to pool in her belly at the erotic slide of his tongue against hers.

He pulled back from her gently, and she ducked her head while she tried to rein in her jerky breathing and slow her skipping heartbeat. After several moments, she peeked up at him and released her clutch on his lapels. "If that's the amuse-bouche, I think dinner will be wonderful."

With a low laugh, he separated from her but grasped her hand lightly, as if a courtier from long ago. His thumb brushed over her knuckles. She'd never thought merely holding hands would make her desire a man. How could she ever have thought him boring?

His features smoothed. "Would you help me with something?"

"Sure." Her brain pushed up her news. "Oh, wait. I'd like to tell you something first."

"Certainly." Eager expectation brightened his features.

"I started clearing out my grandma's room today and got about a quarter of the way through."

"How do you feel?"

The conversation between them returned to her. For some reason he felt…perfect. Like each of the pieces of a puzzle matched to form a clear picture. "It was time. Sometimes the hardest thing to do is begin, you know?"

His features turned enigmatic. "I understand what you're saying."

"Oh, and one more thing." She laid a hand on the fine wool covering his chest. Though she wanted to jump up and down with glee, she limited herself to a simple grin. "I got the job I wanted. The one at the agency in Austin."

His answering smile—one of pure excitement and joy—made her heart want to sing.

"That is wonderful." He enveloped her in quick hug, then released her, framing her shoulders with his hands. "This has been a hard couple of years for you. I know nothing about advertising, but I do know that you will excel at whatever you put your mind to. They're lucky to have you."

The fizziness had turned to full-on bubbles, and she couldn't keep the stupidly happy smile from her features. "Thank you. What did you want help with?"

"First, I have something to tell you too. I want to start fresh. No more security work. I want to build my life. Here. In Texas." His intense gaze seemed to burn a hole into her.

For a split second she mini-panicked. While she wasn't in

love with him, she had a serious case of like. This was way too early to know if she wanted to build a life with him and—

"I've decided I want to study landscape architecture. I looked into a couple of programs and hope to get into the University of Texas."

She couldn't have felt more foolish—or more happy for him. The gardener, Linden, must have had a great influence on him as a child. She put her hands atop his where they rested on her shoulders and gave them an encouraging squeeze. "We have several paranormals on staff in almost all the departments and in the admissions office. I'm sure you'll get in."

Clio wound around her legs with a meow. The torti didn't wait for Tabby to bend down and scratch, she continued to Fernald, who crouched down and lavished attention, much to Clio's delight.

Then he picked her up and put her on the counter next to a wooden box Tabby hadn't noticed before. Clio sat and studied the container, seeming to understand she'd been invited to participate.

The container, slightly larger than a cigar box, appeared worn in a way that spoke of loving use rather than carelessness. Two leather straps kept the lid shut, their buckles glowing more of an ancient brass than the bright gold plate affixed in the middle of the top.

Something had been engraved in the luminous metal, and Tabby bent to get a closer look. A stylized "L." Her hand fluttered to her throat, and she glanced up to him. "Is this what Linden sent you?"

His irises deepened to peacock-blue, and he nodded slowly. "I thought it was time too."

That he would share this with her and Clio made her

insides want to melt. She wrapped an arm around his middle. "I'm honored."

He unbuckled the straps, his movements measured, almost reverent. Did his hands shake a little when he removed the lid? She wouldn't blame him.

Fernald carefully put the top on the counter, then removed a cream-colored envelope bearing his name on the front in a scrawling hand. His pause made her want to urge him to hurry up, but this moment was his. Finally, he broke the forest-green wax seal on the back and pulled out a card.

"*Fernald, sometimes cutting ourselves loose is the best beginning.*"

She'd read along with him, including Linden's signature. "What does it mean?"

"The last time I saw him he answered a question similarly." He brushed aside delicate brown paper and revealed…

A leather pocket of some sort with metal ends poking out.

Fernald stilled, then swallowed hard. He removed the pouch as if the item was the most precious thing in the universe.

After several moments, he tugged on the metal handles. Garden shears slid from the deep pocket. They were a very vintage model, ones with short blades for pruning small branches. She'd found some not all that different in the barn. They were all metal, with a spring between the handles, and a latch on the end to keep them closed. Though in good condition without a smidgeon of rust, the chipped paint and wear on the grips suggested the shears had seen years of use.

Fernald held them spanned across his palms, then he huffed a laugh.

"What's funny?"

He flipped the latch at the end and palmed the handles, squeezing a couple of times. The scissor action operated smoothly and without a squeak. His voice carried a gruff tinge when he said, "I think he knew I would need these someday."

She connected her gaze to his, not at all surprised at the sheen gathering on his lower lids because she blinked back her own tears. Clio bumped her head against Tabby's hand, and she accepted the moment's distraction so she could recover and speak without totally embarrassing herself.

Clio flopped over, her engine running like a revved sports car and her soft belly there to soak up all the love.

The corner of Fernald's lips quirked, and he shot Tabby an amused gaze before he gently stroked the cat's soft fur, earning him a stretch.

Tabby hugged him a little closer to her side. She'd finally cut her ex loose and now stood on the cusp of her own new beginning. The job. Her grandmother's room.

But most important? A new beginning with a gargoyle who was far from boring.

ACKNOWLEDGMENTS

I am sad to say the group of authors behind the Enchanted Rock Immortals world has decided to cease regular releases beginning in 2025. *The Gargoyle Affair* is my last book in this series.

Writing is a strange journey. Often authors find that themes in their lives show up in their stories. One of the themes of this book is starting over. I had almost completed the final edits on *The Gargoyle Affair* before I realized this was my way of cutting loose the Enchanted Rock Immortals and starting anew with an elemental-themed paranormal romance series, hopefully in late 2024.

When Fenley, Eve, Susan, Robin and I began this world during a writing retreat, joined shortly later by Sharla, I never dreamed this would take us on a journey lasting four years. I absolutely could not have written twelve (12!) books without my wonderful partners in crime—they have shown me so much what it means to be part of a team.

Nor could I have climbed this summit without our developmental editor, Dawn Alexander, who made sure my plot holes were paved over and the tension between my characters twanged like a bowstring.

And I absolutely couldn't have done this without you, my reader, part of the faithful clan who not only love my mashup of paranormal romance and romantic suspense, but someone who gives me impetus to keep going. Thank you from the very bottom of my heart.

Wait! There *is* good news here. The author group has reserved the right to release new story content as they see fit beginning in 2025. So you may see a new book release from other world authors.

As for me? Oh, my friends, I want to have some fun.

Occasionally, I will be sending out a chapter via my newsletter that continues one of my stories, but not just any chapter.

That chapter. A sexy continuation chapter for *The Wolf Shifter's Redemption*, or *The Vampire's Vendetta*, or even *The Gargoyle Affair*.

Why weren't these scenes in the book itself? When we conceptualized this series, we put word limits in place to achieve a reasonable release schedule and a consistent experience across all authors' works. For me to complete a mystery, build a rich paranormal world, and create a believable romance arc, I didn't often have the word count to include a sexy scene. I am looking forward to revisiting some of these characters, because I don't have a favorite—I love them all.

Be sure to keep up with me through my newsletter for all the latest news, free stories, and maybe *that* chapter from your favorite Enchanted Rock Immortals book—you can sign up at amandareidauthor.com.

Thank you again for your support and happy tales to you,

Amanda

The Wolf Shifter's Redemption
An Enchanted Rock Immortals Novella
by Amanda Reid

Is this your first Enchanted Rock Immortals story? Check out where Amanda began her series within the Enchanted Rock Immortals world…

Can he convince the love of his life that this wolf needs a second chance?

Veterinarian and animal empath Carrie Fletcher is finally back on track after her parents' murder by a paranormal pure-blood fanatic three years ago. She watched his execution in the arms of Nathan Hebert, a wolf shifter she thought loved her, but dumped her as soon as his mission to protect her ended. Now, it appears the fanatic is back, and so is Nathan. This time the wolf claims he not only wants to keep her alive, he's ready to return her love.

Leaving Carrie had been the worst mistake of Nathan's life, and the shifter's wolf made sure the hole in his heart would never truly heal with the loss of his mate. When he discovers the fanatic he thought long-dead has returned and is targeting the woman he loves, Nathan knows he can no longer deny his fate. Clan Shifter may have hired him and his security team to find and eliminate the fanatic's threat, but now his mission is personal.

Soon, Nathan finds a dangerous conspiracy stretching far beyond the clan, threatening careful balance in the Enchanted Rock Immortals world and the mate he still loves. Not only must he redeem himself by saving Carrie, but convince her that even a wolf needs a second chance.

ABOUT THE AUTHOR

Amanda Reid authors not only Enchanted Rock Immortals urban fantasy romance novellas, but also the Flannigan Sisters Psychic Mysteries, a paranormal cozy mystery series.

Since she was young, she's been a lover of mystery, sci-fi, and paranormal genres. Amanda found her first romance book in her aunt's closet around thirteen years of age and quickly decided it needed to be added to her repertoire.

Beyond writing, Amanda was a career Army brat and lived in exotic locations like Tehran, Iran and DeRidder, Louisiana as a child. She dreamed of a career in the State Department, but ended up as a federal agent. For 24 years Amanda investigated murders, fraud, identity theft, drug trafficking and many other crimes before her retirement. As you can imagine, it's given her a wealth of inspiration for her mystery and urban fantasy stories.

She currently lives in Texas with her husband and two gonzo Australian Shepherds. Click on the icons below to catch up with her on Facebook, Twitter or Instagram. You can sign up for upcoming releases, free stories, and promotions at my website.

amandareidauthor.com

Enchanted Rock Immortals

Made in the USA
Monee, IL
25 November 2025

34763525R00080